Little
Secrets

Nothing but the Truth

Little
Sec

EMILY BLAKE

Nothing but the Truth

Point

If you purchased this book without a cover, you should be aware that this book is stolen property. It was reported as "unsold and destroyed" to the publisher, and neither the author nor the publisher has received any payment for this "stripped book."

No part of this publication may be reproduced, stored in a retrieval system, or transmitted in any form or by any means, electronic, mechanical, photocopying, recording, or otherwise, without written permission of the publisher. For information regarding permission, write to Scholastic Inc., Attention: Permissions Department, 557 Broadway, New York, NY 10012.

ISBN-13: 978-0-439-86721-4
ISBN-10: 0-439-86721-5

Copyright © 2008 by Scholastic Inc.

All rights reserved. Published by Scholastic Inc. SCHOLASTIC, POINT, and associated logos are trademarks and/or registered trademarks of Scholastic Inc.

The text type was set in Utopia.
Book design by Steve Scott

12 11 10 9 8 7 6 5 4 3 2 1   8 9 10 11 12 13/0

Printed in the U.S.A.   40

First printing, July 2008

For everyone who tells the truth . . .
even when it hurts.

Little
Secrets

Nothing but the Truth

Chapter One

"Objection!" the defense lawyer cried, leaping to his feet. "The question is too broad."

"Sustained," the judge said flatly.

Alison felt relief wash over her — she would not have to tell the court what she knew. *Yes,* she thought, answering the prosecutor's question silently. *I have evidence against all of them — my life is evidence!* But now she wouldn't have to say it out loud.

The federal prosecutor looked at Alison and ran a hand over his red patterned tie. "Let's try another tack. Alison, how would you describe your relationship with your mother, Helen Rose?

What is it like to be the daughter of a domestic tycoon and national trendsetter?"

Alison opened her mouth to speak, then closed it again. What should she say? What *could* she say?

Alison turned toward the defense table. Her mother sat perfectly straight in a chocolate-brown Max Mara suit and a light blue scarf that matched her eyes. Her hair was neatly styled and she was "Looking Good" as ever — she could almost have been posing for one of her magazine covers. But her eyes were pleading, no, *willing* Alison to say whatever it took for her to regain her freedom.

How can you expect me to help you when you don't even tell me the truth? Alison screamed in her head. She turned back to the attorney standing in front of her.

"My mother is a brilliant businesswoman," Alison said slowly, "who has ignored me for most of my life. She has built her life around her image as the perfect mother, wife, and homemaker. But it is just that — an image."

There was an audible murmur in the courtroom, and Alison felt a chill. Her testimony was already making an impression. But she had a lot more to say. "She doesn't allow anything to stand in the way of her success — not even her family. Business is her game, and winning is like . . . it's like a drug for her. It means everything. Being my mom doesn't seem to matter that much, unless I do something that makes her look bad."

What she was admitting was awful, but Alison was surprised by how good it felt to tell the truth. She glanced over at her grandmother, who was dressed in a perfectly tailored brown Chanel suit, which contrasted sharply with her white pearls and hair. She nodded ever so slightly at Alison, granting her approval. But Alison was not saying any of this for Grandmother Diamond. She was finally speaking out for herself.

"Alison, do you believe that your mother is guilty?" the prosecutor pressed.

"No. Yes. I don't know what to believe," Alison replied, feeling her shoulders rise.

"Objection! Speculation," Helen's attorney barked.

"Sustained," the judge granted. "Please strike Miss Rose's words," he told the jury.

Alison knew it didn't matter if the testimony was included or not. It had been heard. The prosecutor smiled at her before turning to the judge. "I have no further questions, Your Honor."

Alison avoided her mother's eyes. Helen looked unusually dazed, unusually human.

The defense lawyer was pacing in front of the witness stand. Alison took in his red face and the beads of sweat dripping from beneath his slicked-back black helmet hair.

"Alison," he said gravely. "Do you have any specific reason to believe that your mother is guilty of embezzlement, grand larceny, or tax evasion?"

"No," she admitted.

"And prior to her arrest, did you reside in the same house as your mother?"

"Yes."

"And was she generally present at meals in that household?"

"Yes."

"At bedtime?"

"Usually."

"On weekends?"

"Sometimes."

"Did you ever go to see her at her office?"

"Yes."

"I see," said the lawyer. "So you lived in the same house, saw each other every day, and sometimes visited her at her office. And yet your mother's arrest was a total surprise to you?"

"It was," Alison agreed.

"You were present when your mother was arrested, were you not?"

"I was."

"How did your mother react?"

"She was furious," Alison said. "A bunch of officers had just marched into our home and started taking things. She wanted them to stop."

"Did she suggest that someone was to blame for her arrest?"

Alison paused. She'd almost forgotten that part — but now her mother's angry words echoed in her mind. "She said, 'She's behind this, isn't she?'"

"'*She's* behind this,'" the attorney repeated. "And did you have any idea who 'she' was?" he asked.

"No." Alison looked the attorney dead in the eye. It was the truth. At the time, she didn't.

"And do you now?"

Alison was ready for the question. She didn't flinch. "No," she fibbed quickly.

Her mother's attorney raised his eyebrows. "I have just one more question for you, Alison. Do you have any evidence that would suggest that your mother could be innocent, or that your grandmother, Tamara Diamond, is in any way mixed up in these allegations?"

A buzz ran through the courtroom and the judge rapped his gavel sharply to call for order. Alison glanced at her grandmother but couldn't catch her eye. Beside her, Alison's aunt Phoebe fiddled nervously with her signature pearl necklace, but Tamara herself sat calmly, her posture straight and her expression unreadable.

Alison turned to face her mother. Helen sat so still, it looked like she had stopped breathing. For a brief moment Alison wanted to tell the judge everything — that stuffed under her best friend's mattress were several documents that could prove her mother had been framed and her grandmother was the one who'd done the framing. That even though her mother was guilty of many things — including being a lousy mom — this time, she was innocent.

Alison cleared her throat. She looked back at her mother's lawyer. "No," she lied.

Chapter Two

Alison waited for alarms to go off, for the judge to bang down his gavel and call her a liar. She felt surprisingly tiny and full of guilt for lying on the stands and perjuring herself. But betraying her grandmother was not an option . . . ever.

"You may step down now, Miss Rose," the judge said firmly. Alison looked up at the black-robed man's face, grateful to have finally been excused.

Alison felt a little wobbly as she got to her feet. She hadn't planned to be dishonest. But the question had forced her to decide whom to protect. And the best choice was as clear as the answer she had given on the stand: She had to protect herself.

Keeping her chin up, Alison walked past the rows of gawkers who filled the wooden benches. She looked at no one and did not pause as she made her way toward the door at the back of the courtroom. Behind her, the federal prosecutor announced, "The prosecution rests." Alison pushed open the heavy door and stepped into the wide hall.

The defense will have their chance, Alison told herself. *It might be okay.* But deep down she knew otherwise. Alison gasped for air. She hadn't even been aware that she was holding her breath. Suddenly she felt as if she were suffocating.

Now that it was all over, she was starting to panic. She had just told a lie on the stand, under oath. And her mother might pay for that lie with her freedom.

"Bathroom?" Alison choked out to a custodian who was mopping the floor.

The man pointed to a pair of doors at the end of the hall.

Alison nodded, rushed down the corridor past several carved pillars, and yanked open the door. Inside, all was quiet. A moment of peace.

With shaking hands, Alison turned on the cold water and quickly splashed several handfuls onto her face — a trick her mother had taught her long ago. *"You must always put the right face forward. Never let people know what's really going on inside,"* Alison heard her mother's voice in her head as she looked at herself in the mirror. Icy droplets fell from her face into the basin, and her blue eyes looked back, unsure.

I did it, and I survived, she thought, cupping her hands for another splash. "It was the right thing," she said aloud, trying to convince her reflection. Guilt was seeping in and filling up Alison's heart. But another, stronger emotion was there to push it out: relief. Her testimony was over, and she was still standing.

Taking a final deep breath, Alison shut off the water and ran her fingers through her shoulder-length, layered, brown hair. She was preparing to go back to the courtroom when a stall door opened. X, a girl Alison barely knew from school, emerged wearing an apricot Tocca skirt suit with a white shirt and black tie. It was odd to see her out of the unusual school uniforms she wore to Stafford Academy every day. And it was disconcerting to see her here. The girl seemed to be everywhere.

X met Alison's gaze in the mirror and gave her a sad smile — a look that was sympathetic without being pitying. "Do you ever wonder if there really is a 'right' choice?" she asked quietly.

Alison stared back numbly.

"I mean, the truth can be so subjective," X went on as she washed and dried her hands. "It's really all about point of view. Don't you think?"

Alison tried to smile, as if being caught talking to herself in the bathroom after testifying against her mother was a silly lark. But her forced smile felt more like a grimace.

Suddenly an electronic ring echoed in the tiled room — Alison's phone. Heaving an inward sigh of relief at the interruption, she pulled the phone from her Bottega Veneta bag and glanced at the screen. *Tom Ramirez.*

"Excuse me," Alison said, slipping into the hall to take the call. Her heart was beating quickly. Tom never called her. It had to be about Chad.

"Hello?" she answered breathlessly.

"Alison? Alison, he's awake. Chad is awake!"

"Thank God," Alison said. Relief washed over her and all thoughts of the trial and X vanished. Chad had been in a coma for almost two weeks — the longest days of Alison's life. Finally, finally, Alison would get the chance to tell him that she loved him, too.

"How is he? Is he all right?" Alison asked as she clicked down the marble-floored hall. She was tempted to slip off her heels so she could run — she had to get to the hospital *now* — but there were too many photographers around. She picked up the pace as best she could.

"Tom, how is he?" she repeated.

Tom was silent for a moment longer. When he finally spoke, Alison's heart dropped.

"How soon can you get here?" Tom asked. "Something's wrong."

Chapter Three

Chad Simon looked up at the expectant faces of the people surrounding his hospital bed. Some were in white coats or scrubs with stethoscopes around their necks. Obviously doctors and nurses. Others were in street clothes. But none of them looked familiar. Who were they?

Chad began to panic, a bitter taste filled his mouth. Who was *he*?

Alarmed, Chad struggled to sit up — to do something, *anything* besides just lying there. But when he raised up on his elbows, his arms felt like rubber. *Where am I? What's happening?*

One of the doctors gently pushed him back

down. "Relax, Chad," she coaxed. Chad stared up at her. Who was Chad?

His limbs felt heavy. His head throbbed. Blinking, he tried to refocus, and his eyes came to rest on the stubbly-faced guy to his left.

"Hey, little bro," the guy murmured softly, his dark eyes concerned behind his long curly bangs.

Bro? Chad thought with a start. *As in brother?*

"Chad . . ." A preppier-looking kid — the one who'd been there when Chad first woke up — stared down at him anxiously. "It's me, Tom," the boy said. "Remember?" He was staring at him so intently that it was making Chad uncomfortable.

Chad looked away from Tom and the older kid, away from everyone in the room. He tried to breathe. Their worried faces were freaking him out. And so were the tubes and wires that seemed to be coming out of every part of his body. What was wrong with him? What was he doing here?

That's when he saw her. Standing in the doorway was the most beautiful girl Chad had ever seen. Her geometric-print skirt swirled around her legs just above a pair of knee-high black leather boots. Her long straight blond hair fell over her shoulders and halfway down her back. When Chad met her eyes, she flashed him a dazzling smile. Chad felt that smile from all the way across the room. It made him feel alive and connected. The one bright spot in a sea of headaches and confusion.

Chad wished everyone and everything would go away — except the girl and her smile.

But instead the girl was pushed aside as two more people — a man and a woman — came into the room. Chad looked at the woman uneasily as she rushed straight toward him.

"Oh, Chad," she cried as she wrapped her arms around him. Chad hugged her back gingerly, trying to keep his IV from tugging uncomfortably. She pushed away from him and stared at his face through her tear-filled eyes. "Don't you recognize your own mother?"

Chad squeezed the woman's arms and searched her face for something familiar. Her face was grief-stricken — and totally unfamiliar.

Chad gulped and looked up at the man beside her. He was blinking back tears, too. Chad guessed that the man must be his father.

"It's good to see you, son," the man said.

Chad said nothing. He looked toward the door again. Was the beautiful girl still there? It was hard to see past the crowd of doctors that had suddenly gathered in the doorway. Chad's mother stood up to get a tissue from her canvas bag. His father pushed a button on his bed, raising it so he was sitting more upright.

And then one of the doctors stepped inside. "How are you feeling, Chad?" he asked, dropping his clipboard to his side.

Chad stared up at the gray-haired man. How was he supposed to feel? "I don't know," he said with a small smile. "Maybe you should tell me."

The doctor smiled back kindly. "I see you've retained your sense of humor," he said. Then his tone changed, and he was all business. "Chad, you've been in a coma for almost two weeks. And I probably don't need to tell you that you have amnesia. But there is no need to panic. Memory loss is common among coma patients. It's likely you will regain your memory entirely, but slowly. The best way to help that along is to relax and let it happen. Your brain has undergone quite a shock."

Chad's mother let out a sob and the doctor shot her a "pull it together" look. She sniffled and bit her lower lip.

"I'll be okay," Chad said, wanting to comfort her.

"I'm afraid there's no easy way to say this," the doctor said, turning back to Chad.

There's more?

"So I will be direct," the doctor continued. "Chad, the coma was brought on by an extenuating condition. You have stage two Hodgkin's lymphoma. Cancer of the lymph nodes."

Chapter Four

Kelly stared at her boyfriend from across the hospital room. She focused on Chad sitting half-up in bed. He looked so weak, so vulnerable. Normally that would disgust her. But instead it made her want to go to him, to be strong for his sake. She just had to be near him.

Ignoring everyone else in the room, Kelly walked up to Chad's bed and took his hand in hers. "Chad," she murmured, "I'm so glad you're awake. It's going to be all right. We'll get through this . . . together."

Behind her, Chad's brother Dustin chuckled, and Kelly turned to glare at him. Not a half hour earlier he'd made a fool of her after leading her on for days. But that wasn't why Kelly was annoyed with him. She was irritated because he was questioning her devotion to Chad. Which, at the moment, was completely unwavering.

I'm just so glad he's awake, Kelly told herself, remembering the smile they'd shared a few minutes earlier. That moment was magic. She hadn't felt a connection with someone like that since . . . well, ever.

Kelly smiled down at her boyfriend, and he smiled back. And there it was again — that feeling of connectedness. But a second later an awkward expression clouded Chad's eyes. "I'm sorry — I don't know —"

"I'm Kelly," Kelly said softly. "Your girl-friend."

Chad blinked. His amazing smile widened. "Lucky me," he said, squeezing her hand.

Lucky us, Kelly thought, pulling up a chair to sit down. Chad's mother smiled at her and made room. Chad still had his IV and was hooked up to several other monitors, but Kelly barely noticed. She only had eyes for him. Even though the doctors and nurses, Chad's parents, Dustin, and Tom were all in the room, it felt as if she and Chad were alone. Alone and united.

Kelly leaned in and brushed a blond curl behind his ear. He had such nice, thick hair. "Do you need anything?" Kelly asked. "I could go out and get you —"

"Chad!" Just then Alison burst into the room. Without even taking in the situation, she ran up to Chad's bed and threw her arms around him. "Oh, Chad!" she cried, pulling away and looking anxiously into his eyes. Kelly tightened her grip on Chad's hand, refusing to let go. She glared at Alison through narrowed eyes.

On the other side of the bed Tom inhaled sharply.

"That's me, apparently," Chad said a little woodenly. He looked at Alison, then back at Kelly. His eyes begged for answers.

"Chad, this is Alison Rose," Kelly explained. "My cousin. Your *ex*-girlfriend."

Alison stiffened, and Kelly felt herself relax. Chad was looking to her for answers — and she was giving them. Better still, Alison could not refute them because Kelly was telling the truth. Alison was no longer Chad's girl. She may have dated him for over a year. Chad may even have confessed that he still loved her right before he slipped into the coma. But Chad had no memory of that. It would be Kelly's word against Alison's. Besides, that was then — this was now. And now, everything was different.

It didn't matter who Chad had loved before he'd woken up, or that Kelly had stolen him from Alison in the first place and had been planning to dump him in a flash.

Now that she knew what she had, Kelly had no intention of letting Chad go.

Chapter Five

"Hello? Anybody home?"

Zoey Ramirez slipped out of her thought trance and smiled sheepishly at the guy sitting across from her at Hardwired: Jeremy Jones, her tutor, friend, and major crush.

"Sorry," she said. "I guess I'm a little out of it."

"A little?" Jeremy asked.

Zoey laughed. "Okay, a lot." She looked down at her steaming double mocha. "I just can't stop thinking about Alison," she confessed. "She snuck into her mom's trial today, even though her grandmother told her not to go near it, and she hasn't checked in or answered my texts all day. I'm worried about her."

Jeremy's easygoing expression changed at the mention of Alison's name. He suddenly looked . . . angry.

"What is it?" Zoey asked, feeling uneasy. She knew that Jeremy had been going to the trial, too, whenever his course schedule allowed it. He was a huge Helen Rose fan. "You didn't see her there, did you?"

"Everyone saw her," Jeremy snapped. "She testified."

"She *what*?" Zoey nearly knocked over her mocha.

"She testified . . . *against* her own mother. They called her to the stand and she tore her mom to shreds. Said that Helen has ignored her for her whole life, is cold, calculating, and ruthless, eats kittens for dinner, and kicks babies for fun." Jeremy's blue eyes flashed anger. "That girl has no idea what she's got."

Zoey felt her own temper flare. Jeremy might be obsessed with Helen Rose, but what did he *really* know about Alison, her mom, and the Diamond family?

"Believe me when I tell you that you don't know the half of it," Zoey said flatly. "Do you think she *wanted* to testify? She wasn't even supposed to be there! She must have been terrified. And as for what she said about her mother, what makes you so sure it isn't true?"

Jeremy stared at Zoey, saying nothing. He must have been biting his tongue because his ticked-off expression hadn't changed and he certainly wasn't apologizing. Finally he spoke. "Zoey, she testified against her own mother. What kind of a daughter does that?"

Zoey sighed. Jeremy was the last person she wanted to fight with, and she couldn't betray Alison's trust by explaining what she knew. "Look, Jeremy. It's just . . . complicated." *Really complicated.* All of a sudden Zoey didn't feel right even talking about it. She took a sip of her mocha, grateful that Jeremy stayed silent.

When she put down her drink, Jeremy was staring down at the tabletop, looking miserable.

Zoey was wondering if this was going to be the end of her tutoring sessions when her phone rang. She didn't recognize the number but flipped it open, anyway. "Hello?"

"Zoey, is that you?" The woman's voice on the other end didn't sound at all familiar.

"Yeah, it's me," Zoey replied warily.

"Thank goodness. I wasn't sure if this was the right number. It's Beverly Wilson . . . Audra's mother." Zoey inhaled sharply and felt her stomach drop. Not even two weeks had passed since Audra had fallen to her death — right in front of Zoey. Zoey was still haunted by the gruesome sight in her mind and the guilt at not having stopped Audra somehow . . . even though part of her was relieved that the crazy girl was gone.

"Zoey? Are you there?" Audra's mom asked.

"Yes, Dr. Wilson," Zoey said. "I'm still here."

Glancing across the table, she saw Jeremy's eyes widen.

"Zoey, I have a big favor to ask. I hope it's not too much. I would like to ask you in person. Do you think you could come over? Right away?" Dr. Wilson's voice buzzed in her ear.

Shutting her eyes tight, Zoey wished she'd never taken the call. What could she say? "No" wasn't an option.

"Of course," Zoey heard herself reply. She listened numbly as Dr. Wilson recited the address. "I'll be there in half an hour."

Snapping the phone shut, she looked into Jeremy's sympathetic, questioning gaze. She grimaced. "Can you give me a ride?"

Chapter Six

Jeremy put his hand on Zoey's shoulder. "You sure you want to do this?"

"Do I have a choice?" Zoey forced a smile and tried to look relaxed. "I'll be fine. Thanks for the ride." She hopped out of the sporty black Saab and waited for Jeremy to pull out of the driveway before turning to the house.

The Wilsons' place was big but plain — Colonial style and painted white with brown shutters and a matching brown door. Zoey focused on the gold numbers beside the entry as she walked up the path.

Zoey had barely rung the doorbell when Audra's mom opened the front door wide. "Oh,

Zoey," the tall woman said, holding out her arms. "I'm so glad you've come."

"Uh, me too," Zoey lied as she stepped tentatively into the foyer. Dr. Wilson hugged her tight, then clutched her shoulders and held her at arm's length. "Come inside."

Zoey followed her into the living room, where Audra's dad was sitting on the couch. Even behind his wire-rimmed glasses, Zoey could see his eyes were tired. A giant plate of cheese and crackers sat on the coffee table in front of him.

"Zoey — oh, Zoey!" the other Dr. Wilson cried, getting to his feet. "Thank you for coming." He wrapped his arms around her and pressed her head to his shoulder.

Whoa, Zoey thought, tensing. She hadn't expected the tears and hugging. She knew Audra's parents were both psychiatrists. Maybe that meant they were more in touch with their emotions than, say, a district attorney. . . .

"Would you like something to eat?" Audra's mom offered, reaching for the plate of cheese.

"Yes, thank you, Dr. Wilson," Zoey said, desperate for something to do with her hands. She cut off a chunk of Brie and took a few crackers from the plate before sitting down on the couch beside Audra's dad.

"Call me Beverly," Audra's mom said. "And this is Douglas." She pointed toward her husband.

"We'd really like you to call us by our first names," Douglas confirmed. "Audra did."

Zoey nodded, chewed, and smiled with her mouth closed like there was nothing weird about that.

"I'm sure you're wondering why we brought you here," Beverly said, sinking into an armchair across from the couch, where she could look straight at Zoey.

Zoey nodded again, grateful that her mouth was still full.

"Well, we were hoping that you could tell us about Audra's last moments. You know, before . . . she . . . she . . ." Beverly broke off and looked away.

"Beverly and I . . . we're so sad we weren't able to be with her when she died," Douglas explained. "We know you were there in her last minutes — you had that honor. We're grateful that she wasn't alone . . . that her death did not go unwitnessed." Audra's dad ran his hand through his salt-and-pepper hair. "We were hoping you could . . . Well, can you tell us how she was? Was she happy? Afraid? At peace? Did she want to die?"

Oh, no. Zoey shoved a dry cracker in her mouth and started chewing, slowly. *She wanted me to die,* she thought, nervously chomping the tiny toast to bits and swallowing hard. She could picture Audra lunging at her on the bridge, her eyes murderous. It had been the most frightening moment of Zoey's life. But Zoey couldn't tell Audra's parents *that.* "She . . . I . . ." Zoey fumbled for words and then started to choke on the crumbs in her throat.

"Of course, it must be awful for you, Zoey," Beverly said. She handed Zoey a glass of water. "And the last thing we want is to cause you further distress. It's just that it's so difficult not knowing. . . ." She looked into Zoey's face, her dark brown, almost black eyes welling with tears.

Zoey felt her own eyes moistening and turned away to take a big gulp from the water glass. "I . . . don't know if I can talk about it."

Douglas got to his feet. "Of course. Of course. We're so sorry. Thank you for coming, Zoey," he said kindly. "It was good of you."

"It was nothing," Zoey said softly, setting down her glass and standing to follow him out. She felt sad, and confused, and guilty. And a little bit like she was being dismissed — like the time was up on her therapy session.

"No, it was brave of you." Beverly grabbed Zoey's hand. "And it's so nice to have a girl in the house again. Isn't it, Douglas?" Zoey saw a look of sadness pass between Audra's parents. She wished she could help them.

"Everything has been so . . . empty. I haven't been able to even start going through Audra's room." Beverly pulled a handkerchief out of her pocket and blew her nose quietly. "I'm sorry. It's just . . ."

Reaching out, Zoey touched the woman's arm. "I understand," she said quietly. "When my mother died I felt like my life was over. I had this giant hole, and nothing could fill it up. I still feel sad when I see her things. . . ."

Beverly put her hand over Zoey's. "Of course, your mother. I had forgotten. Of course you understand. Poor thing." She looked at Zoey with hopeful eyes. "I don't suppose you could . . . No, never mind."

"What?" Zoey pressed.

"Perhaps you could come back sometime and we could work on Audra's room together?"

Zoey was too shocked to respond. Agreeing seemed impossible to imagine. But Zoey didn't feel like she could say no, either. So she nodded.

"Wonderful," Beverly said. "How about next Thursday after school?"

Chapter Seven

The next morning Alison got up earlier than usual. She wanted to visit Chad in the hospital, *without* Kelly. She pulled on her favorite pair of Citizens of Humanity jeans and green Ya-Ya sweater and grabbed the photo of her and Chad at the beach last summer that she'd put in a frame on her bedside table after he went into the coma. It was taken back when they were happy and in love — before Kelly had ruined every-thing. Alison ran her thumb over Chad's smiling face before slipping the picture out of the frame and into an envelope. Perhaps seeing the photo would help jog his memory so they could get back to being happy together.

After slipping on her Dior ballet flats, Alison headed down the stairs to grab a bagel from the kitchen. But when she passed the dining room she was surprised to find the table set and her grandmother sitting at the head of it.

"Good morning, Alison," Tamara greeted kindly. Alison stepped into the room and her eyes widened. The table was laid with all of Alison's favorite foods: popovers, scrambled eggs, raspberries, crispy bacon, and fresh-squeezed orange juice.

The smell of the bacon was making Alison's mouth water. Cautiously wondering what her grandmother had to say, Alison pulled out a chair and sat down. A few moments later her plate was filled.

"How did you sleep?" Grandmother Diamond asked as she spooned up a bite of the fluffy eggs.

"Fine," Alison replied. She had, in fact, slept like a baby . . . something she hadn't been doing much of lately. Worry over Chad and the trial had consumed her for what felt like ages. But now that Chad was awake, and she'd done what she had to do in court, she'd slept soundly at last.

"Excellent. You need your rest." Tamara sipped her coffee, then set the gold-rimmed cup back on its saucer. "I'm sorry you've had to suffer through this entire ordeal, Alison," she said. "I know it has been going on far too long. But perhaps this will help." She handed a crisp white envelope across the table.

Setting her glass down, Alison reached for the envelope. Inside was a gift certificate for two all-day treatments at C'est Spa, the poshest day spa in town. Alison smiled grimly. It was so like her grandmother to reward her with something extravagant. *And I deserve it*, she thought.

"Thank you, Grandmother," Alison said aloud.

Tamara nodded. "I thought you could go with the Ramirez girl next weekend," she said. "You deserve a little celebration. The trial is nearly over, and you must be pleased that your friend is no longer in a coma."

Alison blinked in surprise. How did her grandmother know about Chad? She certainly hadn't told her. But it didn't matter how Tamara knew. What mattered was that Chad was awake — and Alison was about to see him.

Chapter Eight

Please remember me, Alison begged silently as she stepped into the elevator at the hospital and pushed the button for the third floor. She'd ridden that elevator and walked down that hall countless times in the past two weeks, but today everything was different. Today Chad would be awake.

"Anybody home?" Alison said quietly as she pushed open the door to room 308.

"Kelly?" Chad called out, sounding excited.

"No, it's Alison," Alison replied as she stepped into view.

"Oh, Alison," Chad said. "Hi." He smiled at her, but it was not a "you're the love of my life" kind of smile. At all.

So much for him remembering everything at the sight of her. Alison plunked the forget-me-nots she'd brought into an empty vase on the windowsill and gave herself a split-second pep talk. *Don't give up,* she told herself as she turned back to Chad. He looked tired. "How are you doing?" she asked, pulling a chair closer to his bed.

"Better," Chad said. "I'm starting to remember things — just like they said I would. But weird things, like my second-grade teacher, Mrs. Sullivan. And that I love chocolate cake. And how I got this scar when I fell off my bike after Dustin taunted me into racing him when I was nine." He pointed to a small scar below his elbow, a slim white crescent next to a smattering of freckles.

Alison looked at Chad's thin face. He was so handsome, with his big brown eyes and curly blond hair.

"That's great," Alison said with a wistful smile. She couldn't help but wish it were *her* he remembered and not Mrs. Sullivan.

Be patient! Alison scolded herself. The boy had just woken up from a coma and now he had cancer. It was so selfish of her to expect things to be like they were before. She shouldn't rush him.

The things she could tell Chad about himself popped into Alison's head. Like how he loved root beer and Redvines at the movies. How he always kept his pencils super sharp. How he hoarded marshmallow Peeps at Easter to eat all year long because he liked them better stale. But if she told him this stuff and he didn't remember it for himself . . . would it mean anything?

I have to try, Alison thought. She reached into her blue Birkin bag and pulled out the envelope with the photo. Before she could open it, the door swung inward and a redheaded nurse appeared. "Time to check your blood pressure," she announced cheerfully. "Oh, hello, Alison. I haven't seen you in a few days. You must be so happy to see Chad awake." The nurse wrapped a black cuff around Chad's arm.

"This girl was here for you every day," she told Chad as she pumped air into the pressure cuff. "Along with Tom — and your parents, of course."

"And Kelly," Chad added with a goofy grin.

Alison flinched but did not correct him.

"One twenty over eighty," the nurse read from the blood pressure dial. "Perfectly normal."

A lump began growing in the pit of Alison's stomach as she watched the nurse take the strap off Chad's arm. He still thought he was in love with Kelly.

"I'll be back in an hour with your meds," the nurse said before she disappeared out the door, leaving Alison and Chad alone once again.

Looking at her lap, Alison stared at the envelope in her hand. This was her chance to explain everything. To say that she still loved him, and that he loved her. And yet . . .

Forget it. Alison shoved the envelope back into her bag. She just couldn't do it. It was weird. Or forced. Or wrong. The boy lying in the bed next to her wasn't the same Chad who had been her boyfriend.

That Chad, *her* Chad, could be gone forever.

Chapter Nine

Tom stepped off the elevator and walked on autopilot toward Chad's room. He was skipping first period — again. But what was more important, history class or Chad? And he couldn't care less what his father or the dean might think. Tom knew he could talk his way around catching any flak at school, so DA Daddy would never have to hear about it, anyway.

Rounding the corner just before Chad's room, Tom almost walked right into Alison. "Oh!" he said as he took a step back.

"Tom. Hey." Alison stopped short, too, shifted her bag on her shoulder, and looked at the floor. Then they both spoke at once.

"I was just —" they both blurted, then looked at each other and laughed.

"You go," Alison said, yielding the conversation. Seeing her smile, Tom felt suddenly nervous, which was kind of weird. He and Alison had spent a lot of time together at the hospital while Chad was in his coma. They'd sat together for hours, studying, reading, and talking. Especially talking. Things had been totally easy and comfortable between them. So why were things so awkward now?

"I'm just going to see Chad before school. Uh, how's he doing?" Tom asked.

"Pretty good," Alison replied. "He's starting to remember a few things."

"He is?" Tom asked. "That's awesome."

Alison nodded but she looked a little sad. "Yeah," she agreed. There was another moment of silence. "Well, I'd better get to school."

"Right." Tom wished she would wait for him but didn't want to ask her to be late. "Catch you later." He stood awkwardly and watched Alison disappear from sight before turning to Chad's door.

"Tom!" Chad greeted him before he was

all the way in the room. Tom's spirits lifted immediately.

"Hey," he said. "How's it going?"

Chad sat up in bed, his brown eyes alight. "That tree house we built in your backyard," he said. "Is it still there?"

Tom smiled. He hadn't climbed up to the tree house for years. "Yup, it's there. Kinda dilapidated, but there."

"Well, I want to check it out. As soon as they let me outta here I want to go see it. Okay?"

Tom shrugged. "Okay," he agreed. It was fun to think about being kids again, but he wondered how soon Chad was going to remember more recent events. There was some stuff that they had to talk about — stuff Chad had to know. And it couldn't wait.

Tom swung a leg over the hospital chair next to Chad's bed and sank onto the green vinyl seat. "Chad, we have to talk," he said, looking his friend in the eye.

Chad nodded, picking up on Tom's somber mood. "All right," he said. "Shoot."

Tom wasn't sure where to begin — there was a lot to say, and none of it would be easy.

"Well . . . when you and Kelly got together, I was really jealous," Tom confessed. He cleared his throat and stared at the nurses' call button. "Right before you, uh, blacked out, we were fighting over her."

Tom forced himself to look Chad in the face. He wanted to do this right.

"Chad, I made a move for her. I tried to steal her from you. I know I was out of line, and I'm sorry." Tom waited for Chad to get angry, to tell Tom to get out of his sight. But Chad didn't look angry. He was smiling. He had been since the first mention of Kelly's name.

"She's really something, isn't she?" Chad said.

"Uh-huh." Tom sat stunned.

Chad reached a hand out to clap Tom's shoulder. "Don't worry about the fight; I forgive you," he said calmly. "Let's just forget it ever happened."

Tom cracked a smile. "Easy for you to say, Amnesia Boy," he joked. Chad laughed. He really seemed okay with it. But Tom still felt unsure. How could Chad *really* forgive him for something he didn't remember? He wanted Chad to fully understand what had happened before he accepted Tom's apology, so they could both know it was real. Losing his best friend again — the one he'd had since they both played starting forwards on their under-eight soccer team — was not an option.

"There are a few other things you need to know, too," Tom said.

"Probably more than a few," Chad joked. But the serious look on Tom's face kept him from laughing.

"You're on scholarship at Stafford, and it's a secret. Your family isn't loaded like Kelly's or Alison's. . . ."

"Or yours," Chad finished, eyeing Tom's layered Penguin polos, True Religion Denim jeans, and Paul Smith sneakers.

"Or anyone else at Stafford," Tom agreed. "I'm the only one who knows you're not a rich kid. Kelly, Alison, all of your other friends — nobody has a clue. You go out of your way to hide it."

"If my tuition is paid, why do I care?" Chad asked, totally serious.

"Because everyone at Stafford cares," Tom explained. "If they knew the truth, you'd be scraping bottom. But you keep it to yourself, and you're total A-list."

Chad was quiet.

"And there's something else," Tom went on. He wanted to get it all out at once. He owed it to Chad to tell him the truth, and to help him hide his secrets. "Almost nobody knows about Will, either."

"They don't?" Chad asked. "Why not?"

Tom shook his head. He felt pretty weird telling Chad all of this stuff, but he was the only one who could. Besides, having all the facts would allow Chad to decide for himself what he wanted people to know and what he didn't. "I think you just wanted to protect him. And yourself."

Chad looked confused and a little sad. "Weird," he mumbled.

"Kinda," Tom agreed. "But it seemed pretty normal before. You're not a bad guy, Chad. You were just looking out for yourself — and your little brother." Tom was wondering if telling Chad all of this so soon had been the right choice. But there was no going back now. "Hey," Tom said, standing up to leave, "I don't want to make you jealous, but I gotta get to chemistry."

Chad raised an eyebrow. "Why would that make me jealous?"

"Dude, it's your favorite class," Tom said, straight-faced.

"It is?" Chad asked.

Tom couldn't keep up the joke. He shook his head. "Not even close." He laughed. "You hate chemistry and it hates you. But look on the bright side — now you've got a great excuse for not knowing the periodic table."

Chad's smile looked only a little bit forced. Even chemistry would be better than a hospital bed.

Tom opened the door slowly. He hoped that when Chad finally remembered Tom's betrayal he would also remember this apology. It might not be much. But it would be something. And Tom hoped it would be enough.

Chapter Ten

Zoey sat in the Silver Spring courtroom with Alison and Tamara Diamond. Helen Rose's defense team had taken less than a week to present her case, and it had only taken the jury one day to reach a verdict. The three of them were waiting to hear it along with about two hundred other people in the packed courtroom. Zoey was anxious and jittery, and Alison was so tense she looked like a statue.

Leaning over a little, Zoey squeezed her friend's hand. She was glad that she could be there for her. Normally her dad was really strict about her and Tom missing school, and supporting a friend wasn't exactly on his list of important things to do. But when he heard that Tamara Diamond herself would be escorting Alison and Zoey to the courthouse, he'd decided she could miss half a day of classes.

Zoey considered trying to distract Alison by telling her about her latest voice mail from Audra's weird parents, but she didn't want to discuss it in front of all these people. And whispering seemed out of the question — Mrs. Diamond didn't allow it. Audra's parents had called Zoey four times since she'd gone over to their house and it had only been a little more than a week. Zoey was dreading going back to help pack up Audra's room, like she'd promised, but in an odd way having contact with the Wilsons was also making Zoey feel better.

Just then the side door to the courtroom opened and Helen Rose was escorted in. Alison turned stiffly to look at her mother, but Helen Rose didn't even glance at them.

Zoey studied the jurors as they shuffled in through the door on the other side of the room. How weird that this group of complete strangers was making a decision about somebody's life — about a lot of lives, really.

"Have you reached a verdict?" the judge asked.

"We have, Your Honor," the foreman replied.

An electric shock traveled up Zoey's spine. The foreman's voice was kind of nasal and carried a Boston accent — and Zoey recognized it immediately. The foreman used to be a receptionist at her father's office. She'd heard his voice every time she called, for years.

With slightly shaky hands, the foreman unfolded a piece of paper and began to read. "We the jury find Helen Rose guilty on all counts of embezzlement, grand larceny, and tax fraud."

Guilty on all counts.

Zoey drew in a breath.

Alison fainted against her.

Chapter Eleven

"Oh!" Alison opened her eyes. Her nose felt like it was burning. Her eyes watered. And she realized she was lying across one of the soft leather seats of the limo, looking across at her grandmother's bony stockinged knees. "What? What happened?" She looked around, confused, and struggled to sit up.

Fernando, her grandmother's driver, offered her a hand. In his other hand he held a bottle of smelling salts. That explained the nose.

She looked out the window. They were parked outside of the courthouse.

With a wave of nausea, Alison remembered

the announcement of the verdict. Guilty on all counts. She must have passed out.

"Shall we go home, ma'am?" Fernando asked Tamara.

"Please, Fernando. Thank you," Grandmother Diamond answered without looking up from the engraved notepaper she had balanced in her lap. Only when Fernando was seated in the front and the window that divided the driver from the passengers was up did Tamara address her granddaughter.

"I trust you had a nice nap," she said calmly.

Still a little out of it, Alison nodded and rubbed her aching head. What did they put in smelling salts, anyway? Her nose was seriously burning. Alison leaned her head against the side of the limo. "Where's Zoey?" she asked.

"I sent her to school — where you would be if you hadn't swooned on us."

Right. Alison stared out the window, watching the bare trees flash past. The sky was late autumn gray — no more honking geese flying by. It was too cold for that, but not yet cold enough for snow. A few pumpkins that had escaped being carved for Halloween brightened porches that were close to the street. As they got closer to the Diamond Estate the houses disappeared, hiding behind tall hedges and wrought-iron fences. Occasional glimpses were all that could be seen from the road . . . a driveway, a pond, a turret. Grandmother Diamond and her neighbors were fond of their privacy.

Slowly Alison felt her brain get back to speed. Maybe she was in shock. She felt numb and exhausted and wished Zoey were there.

Her mother had been convicted. It was over. The trial was finally over — except for the endless reruns in her head. Alison discreetly reached inside her Marni black cardigan to feel the small silver key she wore on a chain. The key was the only thing her father left behind when he'd disappeared a month before. She still had no idea what — if anything — it unlocked, or what her father had meant for her to do with it. But its solidity and constant presence were comforting.

Alison studied her grandmother in the limo. She had her reading glasses on and was adding something to the note in her lap. Tamara was as composed as ever. She looked like she was riding home from the symphony, not from witnessing her oldest daughter become a convicted felon. Grandmother Diamond was unflappable. For Alison, it was reassuring, a sign that life could go on as normal, that there was no need to panic.

She takes good care of me, Alison thought. *She's on my side.* Alison slipped lower in her seat, relieved that it was over.

"There." Tamara closed her pen, took off her glasses, and slipped them both into her slim black Tocca bag. She patted the paper on her lap. Alison lifted her head.

"What's that?" Alison asked.

"The guest list, of course," Tamara said. "For Thanksgiving dinner."

Alison resisted the urge to shake like a cartoon character that has been hit in the head with an anvil. Thanksgiving dinner? Grandmother Diamond was planning a party? Now?

"Things have been so dreary lately. And now that all of this is behind us" — Tamara waved her hand like she was wafting away a bad odor — "we could use a happy occasion."

Alison sat stunned while her grandmother went on talking and tapping on her list with a long finger.

"It's going to be a real family-and-friends celebration," she announced. "Diamond style."

Chapter Twelve

"Four cups?" Chad looked pleadingly at Heidi, his favorite nurse. He had only taken one sip of the sickeningly sweet pink iodine drink, and that had gagged him. Did they really expect him to drink four cups of the awful stuff?

"Sorry." Heidi nodded and gave Chad a sympathetic look. "At least you have an hour to do it," she added. "Good luck. I'll be back to take you to your CAT scan, so don't pour that into the flowers or we'll just have to start over again."

Forcing a smile, Chad held up the drink like he was toasting Heidi at a party. He took a big gulp as the door clicked shut behind her. Blech. He blew out his breath, then chugged as much of the awful liquid as he could. It was not the way he wanted to start the day, but he wasn't interested in dragging out the torture for a full hour, either.

Since he'd woken up from his coma, Chad had gotten his share of torture. He'd been poked and prodded and tested until he was black and blue. His hip was still aching where they had taken a bone marrow sample two days before. But worse than the pain was the waiting. They would not have the test results for almost a week.

At least with this scan they'll see stuff today, Chad thought. He was trying to look on the bright side. But he was quickly finding that there wasn't much of a bright side to Hodgkin's disease — just a lot of tests and some pretty nasty treatment plans.

Flipping on the TV for distraction, Chad ran through the channels. There were no good shows. No good games. He went back and forth between some lame MTV reality show and an even lamer pet show on Animal Planet. Finally Heidi came back to get him.

"You didn't have to get all dressed up for me,"

Heidi joked as she led Chad down the hall to the CAT scan room in his hospital duds.

"Are you kidding? I never go dancing without a gown." Chad tried a dance step but felt a little woozy just walking the short distance down the hall. He was glad Heidi was hanging onto his arm.

"No dancing in here, I'm afraid." Heidi helped Chad lie down on what looked like a small sliding bed. "We need you to lie as still as possible while the red light is on," she explained.

"Arm, please." Heidi took Chad's arm and expertly fitted an IV into the heplock on the back of his hand. When the IV was dripping away, Heidi and a technician pushed Chad into the big CAT scan machine. Chad felt totally closed in — it was like lying in a coffin. Freaky. He tried to breathe normally.

"What if I sneeze?" he asked loudly. Heidi laughed.

"Don't," the technician said. "Ready? Scratch those itches now."

Chad breathed in through his nose. "Ready," he said.

The machine hummed and the red light came on. Chad couldn't move. He couldn't talk. All he could do was lie there and think about all the things that were happening to him — and how scared he was.

Closing his eyes, Chad let images of his past flash by. It was reassuring that he was beginning to remember stuff. But the stuff that came back was the unimportant stuff. And it was coming in little drips like his IV — agonizingly slowly.

His mind drifted to Tom. The Tom from his memories was just a kid, with missing teeth. He was quick on the soccer field, and funny even then. Chad thought about Tom's face now — just the same but with all his teeth and a decent haircut, and something sad hiding behind his wide smile. Chad wondered if the sadness was because of Kelly. Tom had seemed really upset when he'd apologized about their fight. But the troubled look in his eyes hadn't gone away after Chad had told him it was okay.

Chad opened his eyes and saw that the light was still blinking red. The machine was still humming. Shutting them again, he saw Alison's face, sweet and uncertain. Alison confused him.

Heidi had said she sat by his bedside every day while he was unconscious. But according to Tom they had broken up months ago — so why did she care so much? When she'd dropped by, she seemed to be waiting for something from him. But she never said what she wanted, and Chad had no idea what was expected. The truth was, seeing her made him feel uneasy.

Chad had so many questions and so few answers, it was driving him crazy. He wanted to put his life back together, but so many pieces of the puzzle didn't fit: Tom's sadness. Alison's devotion. The lies Tom said he'd been living.

Maybe this is my chance to start over with a clean slate, Chad thought. *Maybe this is my wake-up call.* He had seen a talk show about people with cancer and other life-threatening illnesses coming out of them renewed — with a new lease on life. And he was definitely planning on coming through all of this. He not only wanted to remember what his life was like, he wanted to *live* it. But it would be a long road. His treatment hadn't even started yet — and from what the doctors were telling him, it would be no cakewalk. Hodgkin's disease went throughout the whole body — it wasn't a single tumor they could just cut out.

"Okay, Chad, you can scratch again," Heidi called as the bed began to slide back out of the long machine. Chad stretched as well as he could lying down, sore, and with a needle in his hand.

He noticed that Heidi had brought in a wheelchair for the return trip and was secretly glad. He was exhausted. All he wanted now was to go to bed and sleep all afternoon. He wanted to stop thinking about the big dark cancer cloud hanging over his head. He didn't want to forget — he never wanted to forget anything again, ever. He just wanted to stop thinking.

At room 308 Heidi stepped around the wheelchair and opened the door. "Looks like you have a visitor."

Go away, Chad thought. He was not up for a visit. He leaned forward in the wheelchair to see who it was and his tune quickly changed. Kelly was sitting by the window. His silver lining was waiting for him, and she looked as amazing as he remembered. The slanted afternoon sun streamed in, making her hair glow golden. Turning, she spotted Chad and flashed her killer smile.

"Oh, let me." Kelly stepped around Heidi and pushed Chad into the room. "I came right after school," Kelly said as she leaned over to kiss Chad's cheek. "When you weren't in your room I got worried."

"He's been down at the disco," Heidi joked.

"How are you?" Kelly cooed, ignoring the nurse and helping Chad into his bed.

"Great," Chad answered. And he meant it. "I feel so much better now that you're here. And I have been remembering stuff — not everything, but some stuff."

"I'll leave you two alone," Heidi said. "Don't let her wear you out," she added as she pulled the wheelchair out of the room. Chad waved.

Kelly sat down beside Chad on the hospital bed — which was strictly against the rules — and took his hand. "I missed you," she said as Chad leaned his head back against the pillow. Kelly's eyes widened. "Tough day, huh?"

"I've had better," Chad said, scooting over to give Kelly room. "But let's not talk about my health. Did Alison tell you she stopped by again?"

In an instant Kelly's smile disappeared. Her eyes went dark.

"You don't remember what she did to you, do you?"

Chapter Thirteen

Kelly looked into Chad's worried eyes.

He looked so trusting that Kelly almost felt bad for lying to him . . . almost. But truth could be so difficult to pin down — and there was no way she was going to let Chad slip through her fingers. She was doing it for *them*.

"I hate to have to tell you this," Kelly said, squeezing Chad's hand. "I don't want to see you hurt all over again . . . but you need to know the truth."

Chad listened quietly, waiting for her to go on. Kelly loved the feel of his eyes on her. "The way she dumped you — it was brutal," she said. "It was right after she found out about Will."

"She knows about Will?"

"She found out. She saw you two together one day, and when she figured out he was your little brother, and that he's autistic, she freaked out. She couldn't handle it. She was worried that if anyone heard about Will it would ruin both your reputations. So she dropped you. Right then and there. And she wasn't very nice about it." Kelly watched Chad's face carefully as he processed this news.

Chad pulled his hand away and rubbed his forehead. "Wow. I had no idea. She seems so sweet."

"She can be, if she wants something from someone," Kelly said. The story was sounding so good, she was almost starting to believe it herself. "And I know she regrets losing you. Right after her mom was arrested? She tried to get you back."

"She did?"

Kelly nodded. "We were already together so she started spreading these horrible lies about me." Closing her eyes, Kelly turned away. "It almost worked." Kelly gulped. Then she took a deep breath and reached for Chad's hand again.

He took it and their fingers intertwined.

"Lucky for me, you saw right through her, and the only relationship that ended was my friendship with Alison. She'd been my best friend for as long as I could remember. But the way she treated you . . . the way she treated *us* . . ." Kelly let a tear slip down her cheek.

Chad put his other hand on top of hers. Kelly felt her skin tingle. "I am so sorry you had to go through that," he said, comforting her.

"It's funny," Kelly said with a sigh. "I still miss her sometimes. But I don't think I can ever forgive her for what she did to you . . . to us." Another tear slid down Kelly's cheek. She wiped it away, surprised. That was a real tear. Now that she thought about it, she really did miss Alison. Things had been a little easier — and maybe even a little better — before Kelly had ditched her. But now she had Chad, and not like before. Now Kelly had Chad for keeps.

Leaning forward, Kelly put her head on

Chad's chest. As long as they were together she didn't need anyone else.

"Sometimes I still worry that she'll sneak in and steal you back," Kelly whispered.

"Never," Chad insisted as he wrapped his arms around her. "All of that is over. We have each other . . . forever."

Kelly's eyes closed and she took a deep breath, letting herself believe what Chad was saying. It felt so good to lean on him, to let him take care of her. It felt safe. She could almost forget all her problems at home, and the cancer threatening Chad's life.

But the cozy moment ended when Kelly's phone signaled that she had a new text message. Usually she loved to hear the sound — she'd had a DJ make custom tones just for her. They were so catchy they made her want to get up and dance. Right now the sound made her want to throw her phone across the room. Annoyed, she fished it out of her pink crocodile LAI bag.

When she read the name on the screen her annoyance turned to rage. Truthteller! That blackmailing runt had left her another text message.

I SEE YOU W/ HIM. PAY UP.

$1K TO PO BOX 321

Kelly felt her face go red and snapped her phone shut. Her blackmailer had to be Zoey Ramirez — she'd seen Kelly and Dustin together at Hardwired, a while back, and she was exactly the type of loser to pull this kind of stunt. Did she really expect Kelly to give her money? It was time for this little bug to get squashed.

"What is it?" Chad asked.

"Nothing." Kelly shoved her phone deep in her bag and forced her angry expression back to normal. *Absolutely nothing,* she repeated in her head. Zoey was a nothing, and nothing was exactly what she was going to get. She had nothing on Kelly this time. That Dustin thing was so over — Chad was clearly the one for her.

"Hey, little bro!"

The door to room 308 opened and a familiar shaggy head poked in. Kelly gulped as Dustin took off his Diesel sunglasses and sauntered into the room.

"Why, Ms. Reeves, what an unexpected bonus."

Chapter Fourteen

Dustin crossed the room in two long strides and leaned up against the windowsill, making himself at home with the fading bouquets. There were a lot of them, he noted. His little brother obviously had a fan club. And there, on the bed, was the honorary president. But Kelly Reeves looked uncharacteristically nervous. She was digging around in her bag for something as if her life depended on it.

"Looking good, Chad." Dustin flashed his little brother a smile. In truth he looked pretty terrible — pale and weak. The cancer tests were definitely taking a toll. But Dustin was grateful that Chad was awake. He didn't always show it, but he loved his brother. Besides, losing their golden child would probably make his parents expect more from him — the black sheep of the family. Not that he didn't fully intend to prove them wrong. Dustin was going to make it, and make it big. How nice that Kelly was there to hear about it, too.

"I just wanted to come by and tell you the good news," Dustin said, walking around to the other side of Chad's bed. "I stumbled upon this amazing investment deal — a construction thing — and I have a great opportunity to get in on the ground level."

He paused to give them a chance to respond, but nobody said anything. Dustin crossed his arms over his chest and watched Kelly smear some glossy stuff on her lips.

"I just have to gather enough capital, you know?" he went on. "If I can secure the capital, I can get a loan." He eyed Kelly. She was a capital kind of girl.

"That's great!" Chad said with an enthusiastic smile. He looked like he meant it, too. "I hope it works out for you."

"Yeah, me too," Dustin agreed. He shoved his

hands into the pockets of his distressed jeans and let out a snorting laugh.

There was a light knock on the door and it opened. "Time for meds." A red-haired nurse came in smiling and holding a small paper cup with two pills. "Just ibuprofen, for the sore hip," she explained.

"No chemo yet," Chad explained with a yawn. "They're saving the good stuff for later."

Dustin laughed but knew better. Chemo drugs were a drag. He just hoped his little brother could keep his sense of humor during his treatment — he'd need it.

"Looks like you're getting a little worn out," the nurse said. "It's been a long day. Maybe it's time for your friends to go home." She raised an eyebrow at Kelly and Dustin.

Dustin was ready to get out of there — he needed caffeine and some air. But he wanted a little more time with Kelly . . . alone.

Dustin slipped his aviator sunglasses back on and turned to Chad. "You don't mind if I borrow your girl for an hour, do you?" Dustin didn't wait for Chad to answer before turning back to Kelly. "You look like you could use a cup of coffee."

Kelly looked from Chad to Dustin and back. Dustin could tell she was falling for it.

"She's all yours," Chad replied with a drowsy smile. "But you'd better take good care of her."

Kelly stood up and kissed Chad on the cheek. "Sweet dreams," she whispered.

Dustin smiled. It was time to play his hand.

Chapter Fifteen

"It's totally bizarre," Zoey confessed, leaning across the table toward Jeremy during her Friday afternoon tutoring session at Hardwired. "I mean, you'd think being at Audra's house would be totally creepy. But it's actually kind of nice."

"Nice?" Jeremy echoed, raising an eyebrow.

Zoey nodded. She hadn't really planned on talking about the Wilsons with Jeremy, but her visit with them yesterday was on her mind. And it was way better than talking about the Helen Rose verdict. Jeremy was obsessed.

"Uh-huh. Her parents are good people. And

seeing all Audra's stuff . . . I mean, it's weird, but she doesn't seem so crazy anymore."

"Maybe that's because she's dead," Jeremy said pointedly. "She's not around to do anything nuts, like stalk you or push you off bridges. You and your brother are both safe from her craziness."

"I know. I know. But . . ." She pushed her bangs out of her face. "There's a lot of stuff I didn't know about Audra. Like she went to boarding school a few years ago, too. Her mom said she got really homesick and they let her come back after a week. When I got homesick my dad told me to buck up, that being away from home was 'character building.' As if my mom dying when I was ten wasn't character building enough. . . ."

And speaking of things that had to be endured . . . Zoey flinched involuntarily as the door of Hardwired swung open and Kelly came into the café with a scruffy-looking guy around Jeremy's age who looked vaguely familiar. Hunching down in her seat, Zoey tried not to stare. Maybe the Barbie wouldn't notice. She was usually too wrapped up in herself to see anything else. But Kelly spotted her immediately and stomped up to their table, her green eyes shooting daggers.

"Game's up, Ramirez. You lose. I'm not giving you another cent," she hissed through her perfect white teeth.

Huh? Zoey stared at her. "What are you talking about?"

"Come on," Kelly scoffed, "we both know you're blackmailing me — and it's not going to work. Dustin is my boyfriend's brother, and we have nothing to hide. I would never hurt Chad."

Zoey laughed, hard. She couldn't help it. Kelly would hurt *anyone* — she lived to cause pain. Alison was living proof! "You're being blackmailed, and you think I'm doing it?" Zoey shot back as soon as she caught her breath. "Sorry to disappoint, but I have better things to do than waste my time on you. And as far as you sparing the feelings of Chad — or anyone — who are you kidding? Everyone you touch ends up broken or bleeding."

"Well, at least they're alive," Kelly sneered.

Zoey pushed back her chair and jumped to her feet so quickly that Kelly had to step back. Zoey stepped up until they were almost nose to nose. "I did not kill anyone," Zoey growled. "But it's never too late to start. So *step off.*"

Kelly didn't move an inch. "What'll you do, light me on fire? Push me off a bridge? Call your daddy? Do you think he'll help you if you promise to vote for him?"

Ouch. Zoey had to work hard not to show any reaction to that one. She had to hand it to Kelly — she always knew which buttons to push.

Over Kelly's perfect blond shoulder, Zoey saw Chad's brother walking toward them carrying a steaming latte and a large coffee. She wished she could toss one in Kelly's face and scald the smirk off it.

"Here you go, Reeves." Dustin handed over the drink topped with foamed milk. Totally oblivious to what was going on, he smiled at Zoey and Jeremy. "Aren't you going to introd —"

"Not today." Kelly interrupted Dustin without taking her eyes off Zoey. "This isn't over,

Ramirez," she promised. Then, turning on her red Casadei boot heel, she strode to another table. Dustin shrugged and followed.

Fuming, Zoey sat back down. The queen bee had landed a good sting. And worse, she'd gotten the last word.

Chapter Sixteen

Kelly flipped her hair over her shoulder and took a sip of her skinny latte. There! Not only had she silenced the pyro, she'd also embarrassed her in front of her boyfriend — the one who was still looking this way.

Sorry, I'm already taken, Kelly thought with a grin. Jeremy was pretty cute in his Lucky jeans and leather jacket, but nobody compared to Chad.

Chad! Kelly got a warm, fuzzy feeling just thinking about him. He was so adorable — and strong. Before he'd gotten sick, Kelly'd had no idea he was so brave. In a way Chad's cancer was the best thing that had happened to them.

"Your brother is amazing," Kelly said, turning to Dustin.

Dustin nodded thoughtfully. He was leaning back in his seat drinking his coffee and looking around the café. His button-down shirt was open over a vintage screened T-shirt, and his sheepskin-lined coat was slung over the back of his chair. His left leg jiggled under the table.

"You're so lucky to have him," Kelly added.

"I am," Dustin agreed, leaning in to rest one elbow on the table. "And so are you. I'm glad you two kids are still together. I just wish I could do more to help him. It's going to be a long road. . . ."

He paused for a minute, meeting Kelly's gaze across the table before looking back down at his hands. "It's tough knowing I won't be able to be there for him the whole time since I have to leave town for my job. If I could just get in on the ground level with this investment thing, I could make a difference. I could really help. . . . I just don't know how to tell him that I can't be there when he needs me." He trailed off, looked away, and took a sip of his coffee.

Kelly got a sick feeling in her stomach at the mention of Chad's treatments. She didn't like to think of Chad suffering. "What about your parents?" she asked. Hers were the first place she'd go if she needed money.

Dustin shook his head. "Ever since they kicked me out . . . well, I just can't ask them. This is something I want to do on my own . . . for Chad."

For Chad. Kelly nodded, understanding completely. There wasn't anything she wouldn't do for Chad. "How much do you need?"

"Ten grand," Dustin replied casually. Then he looked at her sharply. "But Kelly, I'm not ask-ing . . . I'd never —"

"Ten thousand," Kelly repeated quietly, cutting him off. It was a small price to pay to help the guy she loved. "Ten thousand it is," she said.

Chapter Seventeen

The next morning Chad lay in his hospital bed staring out the window. He'd just gotten his CAT scan results back, and the news wasn't good. The doctors were going to have to go for a pretty aggressive treatment. Outside, a pair of squirrels was playing chase. They seemed so carefree.

And you will, too, Chad told himself determinedly. Whatever he had to go through — whatever he was up against — it wouldn't last forever. And pretty soon they'd let him go home. He would have to come back for his treatments, but at least he wouldn't have to live there anymore. Getting out of the hospital — away from all the illness and that sick smell — would be a good start. He was going a little bonkers being cooped up twenty-four/seven. If it weren't for the almost continuous visits from his family and friends, he'd go completely nuts. . . .

Chad pushed a button on the side of his bed to raise it a little. Maybe if he was high enough he could see the sidewalk — see regular people walking around outside.

Chad was craning to see the ground when the door opened and a beautiful girl walked in. Chad drew a sharp breath as he took in her almond-shaped eyes, straight black hair, and mysterious smile. She was dressed in a pale blue top, pattern skirt, and black boots.

"It's good to see you sitting up, Chad," the girl said, smiling warmly and crossing to the bed. "You look better than you did the last time I visited. Much better." Chad felt a little uneasy at the thought of this girl seeing him in a coma.

"I'm sorry, I don't know who you are," he admitted. He didn't even consider acting like he remembered her. What would be the point?

"Of course you don't," the girl agreed. "We go to school together, or did. But I'm pretty new to Stafford, and we've never actually spoken. I'm X."

She held out her hand, which had several silver rings on two of the fingers. They matched the stacked silver bangles that jangled softly on her slim wrist.

Chad took her hand a little cautiously. If they had never actually spoken, what was she doing here? And what kind of name was X?

"X? Is that your name?" he asked.

The girl laughed. "No, not really. My real name is Alexa. Alexa *Singh*. But apparently three syllables was way too long, so Alexa got shortened to Lexi, and then Lex. Now it's just X."

Chad stared at the girl, studying her face. She had beautiful, wide-set brown eyes and long eyelashes. And a good sense of humor. But there was something unnerving about her. "So you go to Stafford?"

X reached out to smooth the furrow on his brow. "Don't worry so much, Chad," she said lightly. "I'm not like most girls at Stafford. In fact, I'd say I'm precisely unlike them." She glanced around the room. "But never mind that now," she said. "Let's talk about you. When are they letting you out of here?"

Chad watched X toss a large wilted bouquet into the garbage. She held up the vase of slimy water. "The flowers are so beautiful, but they rot so quickly stuck in a glass," she said with a sigh.

"I'm going home for Thanksgiving," Chad said, ignoring her weird comment. Who *was* this girl?

"Perfect," X said as she turned for the door. "That'll be just in time. We're all rooting for you, you know."

Chad watched X disappear through the door without saying good-bye and felt even more confused. Just in time for what?

Chapter Eighteen

Now this *I could get used to,* Zoey thought. She leaned back in the spa chair enjoying her acupressure foot massage. Trance music and the sound of running water created a soothing atmosphere as a team of aestheticians attended her every need. She and Alison had already had their therapeutic mineral baths and hot stone treatments. Now they were wrapped in hot herbal towels to detox their skin. Periodically a spa tech offered them sips of sparkling lemon water for hydration. Special ginseng masks covered their faces and they had cucumber slices over their eyes. After this, a regular pedi at the downtown nail salon was going to pale in a big way — even if they got the good leather massage chairs.

"I'm just so glad it's over," Alison whispered from her recliner to Zoey's left. "Grandmother Diamond and I are getting along so much better now that the stress of the trial is gone, and even though I feel a little guilty for my mom, I know I did the right thing for me."

"Which nobody else seems to be doing," Zoey pointed out.

"Exactly," Alison agreed. "I miss my dad, but at least now I have a way to write to him. And who knows? Maybe he'll come back relatively together and we can start over with my grandmother on our side. As weird as it sounds, having my mother's trial over and her out of the picture for the foreseeable future makes things simpler."

"What about Chad?" Zoey asked softly, resisting the urge to throw off her veggie slices and sit up so she could see Alison's face. She didn't want to ruin her towel wrap.

Alison sighed. "That's the hardest part right now. All this cancer stuff is just so scary — it doesn't even seem real. But I'm hopeful. I mean, his memory has to come back eventually, doesn't it? I just have to be patient and know that someday he'll remember how much we care about each other. Oh, and I'm going to visit him again, in case that triggers something. I'm going to the hospital right after this."

"Good. We don't want Kelly to get her talons too far into him," Zoey said. Then she sat up straight, not caring about her cucumbers or her hot towels. "Oh my god! I can't believe I forgot to tell you!" she practically shrieked.

Alison pulled off her own cucumbers and blinked. "What? What? Tell me!"

"Kelly is being blackmailed!" Zoey said, thrilled to spread the news.

"No way!"

"Totally. And she thinks *I'm* the one doing it. She made a huge scene over it in Hardwired."

Alison giggled and let the spa techs push her gently back down in her lounge chair so they could adjust her wraps. "Wow. I wish I could have been there for that. Who do you think is doing it?" she asked. "I mean, her number one enemy fell off a . . ." She looked at Zoey sheepishly. "Sorry," she said quietly. "I know you —"

"It's fine, Al," Zoey said. Audra's death was an unavoidable fact. "Actually, hanging out with the Wilsons is really helping me deal with all that stuff. I was over there Thursday helping her mom clean out her room, and they asked me to stay for dinner. It was kinda weird at first, but then it was like . . . I don't know. Nice. I mean, they asked me about my day and actually listened to my answer. They ask lots of questions — I think because they're shrinks or something. And they're just so grateful to have me there, to have a kid in the house again. They treat me like one of the family."

"Do you think they are trying to turn you into her — I mean, make you their new daughter?" Alison asked.

Zoey laughed. "This isn't a soap opera, Alison. I think they're just looking for closure. And as refreshing as it is to interact with adults who actually care about my life, I've got enough to handle with my own parentals."

Alison sighed and put her cucumbers back on her eyelids. "You and me both."

Chapter Nineteen

Hydrated, polished, massaged, and refreshed, Alison sat in the chair next to Chad's bed, studying his face. Chad looked exhausted, pasty, and weak.

Maybe I should wait to talk to him another time, Alison thought. The conversation was going to be pretty heavy. Her emotions were crashing around inside her like ocean waves in a storm. But it would be better to get some of this stuff out in the open — sort of a mental detox and resurfacing.

"Chad," Alison said softly, looking him in the eye. "There's something I need to tell you," she paused, "about us."

Chad turned to face her directly. She hadn't seen such intensity in his face since . . . well, since he'd confessed that he still loved her. "I already know," he replied. "And I think we should let it go. Move beyond that. What's past is past. It's over."

Alison swallowed what she had planned to say and turned away so that Chad wouldn't see her eyes welling up with tears. How could he so easily say it was over?

"Let's just forget all that and start over . . . as friends," Chad added more gently.

Alison looked back at him and smiled sadly. He'd said it. The "F" word. *Friends.* That was what he wanted them to be. That, and nothing more.

Ugh. Why was this so hard? A small part of her knew that Chad was right, that starting over as friends would be the best way to erase the lies and weirdness between them and begin again. But she still longed to wrap her arms around him and never let go. "It's probably for the best," she agreed, trying in vain to keep the sadness out of her voice. The sense of loss she felt was overwhelming. Chad nodded.

"So, are you excited to be going home?"

Alison asked, changing the subject while she blinked back tears. Distraction was probably the best medicine — at least for the moment. "I'll bet Will can't wait for you to be back."

Chad openly glared at her — something he'd never done. "Leave Will out of this," he said hotly. The fire in his eyes was frightening.

"I'm sorry," Alison said, recoiling. "I didn't mean —"

"In fact, I'd prefer it if you didn't mention his name again — to me or to anybody," Chad practically hissed. There was some color returning to his cheeks, but it wasn't a healthy glow. It was rage.

"I didn't —"

"Ever." Chad said this last word so bitterly that Alison nearly broke down on the spot. She felt utterly confused. What did she say? What just happened? Who had Chad become?

"Okay," Alison agreed, scooting farther away like a puppy with its tail between its legs.

"Good."

Whoa. Unsure of what to say next, Alison looked around the room. Her eyes stopped on the bouquet of forget-me-nots she had brought a few days earlier sitting on the windowsill. They were withered and colorless, dead . . . just like her relationship with Chad.

"Can I get you anything?" she asked, still not meeting his gaze. Chad must have been feeling sick and tired. That was the only way to explain his harsh words. "I'd be happy to —"

"No thanks," Chad said, interrupting her. His voice had lost its nasty edge, but the cold emptiness that had replaced it was just as painful to hear. "I have everything I need."

Turning her head back to look Chad in the face, Alison was speechless. Was that supposed to mean he didn't need her? His eyes were blank. Alison couldn't tell, and she couldn't take any more.

"Well, I guess I'll go then," Alison said, getting to her feet and grabbing her embroidered jacket off the back of the chair. She wanted to get out of there before she started crying.

"Thanks for coming," Chad said without emotion. Alison had no idea if he meant it or not.

"Sure." Alison smiled through watery eyes. This time she didn't bother to wipe the tears away. Like everything else, it seemed pointless.

Turning, Alison hurried out the door and down the hall. When the elevator doors closed, she slumped against the wall. Chad didn't love her anymore. He didn't need her, either. And he definitely didn't want her.

Alison felt as rejected as she had when Chad had dumped her the first time — worse, actually. Because this time, Kelly hadn't put him up to it. This time, Chad had decided for himself.

The elevator stopped on the ground floor. Alison headed outside holding her jacket in her hands, too numb to feel the cold. The gray sky mirrored her somber mood.

I used to feel so great after visiting Chad, she thought. *Like I never wanted to leave.* Today she hadn't been able to get out of there fast enough. *Things should be better with Chad awake, not worse.*

Alison inhaled the cold air sharply and stopped in her tracks as she realized what the difference was. When Chad was in a coma, she wasn't really spending time with him. She'd spent all of those hours and afternoons talking and laughing and crying with someone else.

Tom.

Chapter Twenty

Tom eyed the leafless tree branches outside through the glass roof of the pool atrium. The indoor/outdoor space ran along the back of their house. In the summer they slid open large paneled walls so the pool was open to the yard. In the winter the panels were closed, but the cold air still found a way inside. Shivering, Tom slipped out of his robe. Taking a swim had seemed like a good way to start his Sunday when he was still in bed, but at the moment he was seriously questioning his sanity.

Sliding his goggles onto his face before he had a chance to change his mind, Tom dove into the long deep-blue tiled lap pool. The water was freezing thanks to the broken heater that he hadn't yet told his dad needed repairing — that would require actually speaking to him — but Tom ignored it and the goose bumps rising on his arms and legs as he swam an easy freestyle to the other end and did a flip turn. It always felt great to get back in the water, no matter what the temperature. It would be good when swim team started up again and he could get into the heated, Olympic-sized pool at Stafford. In a few weeks the Ramirez's lap pool would be better for ice-skating.

Tom dolphin-kicked toward the other side. A few powerful butterfly strokes and he was on his way back again, and feeling a little warmer, too. As he rose up out of the water he thought about last night's announcement. It hadn't been a month since the wedding and already DA Dad was proceeding with the next spectacle — a no-holds-barred congressional campaign launch party. Tom kicked faster, flipped, and pushed off the wall, hard. The last thing he wanted to deal with was another one of his father's "shows" to perform at.

Unless I don't perform . . . Tom thought as he went back to freestyle and took a side breath. Maybe the launch party would be the perfect place to turn the spotlight on his mother's death — and his father's involvement in it. The page from his mother's psychiatric file that Audra had stolen for him was cryptic at best, but it definitely showed that Susan Ramirez had been afraid of her husband. That, combined with the photo he'd found of his dad's car on the scene was all the proof Tom needed. With a little planning Tom could launch a campaign of his own.

After several more laps Tom climbed out of the pool and donned his robe and flip-flops. Shivering, he hurried to the back door and into the kitchen. He was starved.

Tom grabbed a bowl out of one cupboard and a box of cereal out of another.

"Hi, Tommy," his stepmother, Deirdre, chirped. She had her face buried in the refrigerator and handed Tom the milk carton without turning around. "Did you have a nice swim?"

"It was cold," Tom replied, "thanks to the broken heater."

"The heater is broken?" Deirdre asked, briefly turning to Tom before she resumed her search.

"Been broken for months," Tom replied.

Deidre shook her head as she emerged with a Saran-wrap-covered plate of leftover chicken. "Your father might be a brilliant politician, but he is terrible at managing things around the house. I'll call someone and get it fixed — otherwise we're going to have to start calling you little Boy Blue!"

Ugh. Right. Tom cringed and nodded as he spooned up a giant bite of Cap'n Crunch. It would be good to swim in eighty-degree water again. He watched as Deirdre set the plate of chicken on the counter and attacked it with a fork and knife.

"You sure you want that for breakfast?" he asked, eyeing the pieces of cold cooked bird warily. It was a big change from her usual diet shakes and carob bars.

Deirdre giggled and put down her fork just as Zoey came into the kitchen. Ignoring both of them, Zoey grabbed a glass from the cupboard and started to fill it with water from the refrigerator door.

"I'm having the strangest cravings," Deirdre confessed, her eyes bright with excitement. "Your daddy didn't want me to spill the beans yet, but I'm too excited to keep it a secret. You're going to have a new brother or sister!"

Tom choked on a bite of cereal. "What?"

"I said, you're going to have —"

Tom held up his hands. "I heard you," he said.

Zoey's glass overflowed, spilling water onto the floor. She was staring at Deirdre with a mixture of hatred and disgust.

And then Deirdre's eyes went wide and her face went white. Covering her mouth with her hand, she raced out of the kitchen to the nearest bathroom. Tom heard the door slam and then . . . *Oh, gross.* Deirdre was heaving up the chicken she'd just scarfed down.

Tom grimaced.

Zoey sucked in her breath, covering her mouth with her hand. She looked like she might start barfing any second, too.

Chapter Twenty-one

Kelly glared across the dining room table at her cousin, who was smirking over some shared joke with their grandmother — a joke Kelly knew nothing about. They were leaving her out on purpose and Kelly knew it. Ever since Aunt Helen had been convicted, Alison and their grandmother had been thick as thieves — which made Sunday brunch at the Diamond estate even more irritating than usual. Kelly despised being reminded of her not-the-favorite-granddaughter status.

"May I be excused?" Kelly asked, forcing a smile and eyeing her grandmother at the head of the table. Dressed in a camel-colored suit and sitting as erect as a telephone pole, Her Highness looked as in control as ever.

"I suppose," Tamara replied with a small nod.

Kelly was on her feet in an instant. She didn't even bother to clear things with her mom and dad, who were still sipping their cappuccinos. At Grandmother Diamond's house, her parents relinquished what little authority they had.

Kelly left without saying good-bye. She had places to go and people to see — one person in particular and not the usual one. Today it was Dustin. He and Kelly had made a plan to meet at Hardwired so she could get his bank info and transfer the money he needed to his account.

Outside, her driver, Tonio, was waiting. He opened the door and Kelly hopped into the backseat of the large black SUV. The sooner she got away from this place, the better.

"Hardwired," she told him.

Tonio stepped on the gas, speeding out of the driveway. Kelly smiled. She and Tonio had a few things in common. They both liked to move fast.

Ten minutes later Kelly's car screeched to a halt outside the café. Kelly was just about to open the door when her phone beeped. Tt. Again.

Two-timer. Where's the $$?

My price is going up.

Send 2k today.

Kelly hit delete. Zoey could check that mailbox a thousand times. Kelly wasn't paying, now or ever.

"I'll deal with you later," Kelly murmured as she opened the door to the café. Dustin was already at a table waiting with two coffees. He scooted one across the table when Kelly sat down. "Nonfat latte, right?" he asked.

"Right," Kelly replied with a smile. It felt good to be doing something for Chad. She sat down and pulled out her LifeDrive Palm. "The money is all set to go, but I need your account info."

Dustin took his cell phone out of his pocket and laid it on the table along with his keys. Finally he pulled a scrap of paper from his pocket. "Here it is," he said, pushing the scrap toward her. "When will the money be there?" he asked. He sounded anxious. "You said ten grand, right? Or was it fifteen?"

Kelly took a sip of her latte and gave him a hard look. "Ten," she said flatly. "I'll do the transfer today."

"Ten, right," Dustin repeated. He gulped his coffee down and stood up. "Thanks, thanks a lot, Reeves," he said. "I knew I — that Chad and I could count on you."

Kelly smiled at the mention of Chad's name. "You're welcome."

"All right, then," Dustin said, rapping his knuckles on the table and swooping up his keys. "Catch ya later?"

"Sure," Kelly replied with a shrug. She watched the older Simon brother leave, feeling satisfied. She had no interest in Dustin as a boyfriend anymore, but it still felt good to have him in her debt.

Kelly got to her feet. Now that she'd taken care of this, she could go see Chad at the hospital. She was turning to go when she noticed Dustin's cell phone still sitting on the table. Kelly picked it up. She considered going after him with it, then changed her mind and dropped it into her purse. She was no delivery girl. If Dustin wanted it back, he could come to her.

Chapter Twenty-two

On Monday morning Zoey and Tom took a cab to school together. As the yellow sedan rolled down the streets of Silver Spring, Zoey brought up the horrible yet unavoidable reality of Deirdre's bombshell.

"I hope it's a boy," Zoey said seriously. "Otherwise the poor kid will be so swaddled in lace she'll never learn to walk."

Tom let loose a laugh. "And don't forget the pink feathers!" He cringed.

"Ugh, feathers!" Zoey dropped her head in her hands, remembering the hideous, feather-covered bridesmaid dress she'd had to wear at her father's wedding. Just thinking of it made her nauseous.

"Imagine the nursery," Tom said. "It'll be one-hundred-percent Pepto Bismol. I'm talking pink crib, pink rug, pink curtains, pink diapers, pink —"

"Stop!" Zoey gasped, holding up her hands. Her eyes were watering from laughing so hard. "Turn off the pink!" She wiped her eyes, and the humor of it all was wiped away as easily as her tears. "For real. This will all be happening before we know it. And I, for one, don't want to get saddled with taking care of the brat." There. She'd said it aloud.

Tom eyed his sister. "And why would you?"

"Come on — you think Dad is going to change diapers? It's not like he changed ours. And Deirdre will have her precious nails to worry about."

"Don't worry," Tom said. "I'm sure they'll hire a whole squad of nannies. Besides, we shouldn't be so selfish. We really should be happy for Dad — now he'll get a shot at having the perfect child he has always wanted."

Zoey grimaced as the cab pulled up in front of Stafford. "You mean his clone?" she griped as Tom handed the driver a twenty. They got out and hurried toward the main entrance to Stafford. It was cold enough for her to see her breath, and she'd forgotten her scarf.

"Yeah, his clone," Tom echoed with a hollow laugh as he pulled open the door.

Suppressing a shudder, Zoey stepped inside the warm school building. "I gotta go to the office," she said, jerking her head down the hall to the left.

"What for?" Tom asked. "You in trouble again?" he ribbed.

Zoey briefly considered lying to her twin. She couldn't do it. They'd only recently reconnected, and Zoey didn't want to jeopardize that — especially since Tom was one of the few people in Silver Spring she could trust. "For the Wilsons," she said, coming clean.

A flash of guilt crossed Tom's face, followed by a look of utter astonishment. "What are you doing for the Wilsons?"

"They want to start a scholarship in Audra's

name, and I told them I'd bring them some info about it."

"You're going to her *house*?" Tom pressed, giving his sister an "are you insane" look.

"Yeah. I've already been a couple times, okay? They just want a little help, and some info . . . and they're hurting, Tom. You remember what it was like after Mom . . ." She looked into her brother's eyes and saw them soften. "It's too hard for them — cleaning out Audra's room and all. So I said I'd come by . . ."

"Did you know that Dr. Wilson was Mom's shrink?" Tom blurted.

"What?" Zoey gasped. "Which one? Are you sure?"

"Positive. It was Audra's dad."

Zoey felt a chill run up her spine. Douglas Wilson had been her mom's shrink. Her doctor. The person she had told her deepest, darkest secrets to before she . . .

Whoa.

Chapter Twenty-three

Clutching the scholarship fund paperwork to her chest, Zoey knocked on the Wilsons' front door late Monday afternoon. All day long she'd been thinking about the fact that Audra's dad was her mother's psychiatrist. And the more she thought about it, the more it freaked her out. How long had she seen him? What had they talked about? Did her mom talk about her? Did Dr. Wilson know just how depressed her mother was? Had he tried to help?

Audra's mother opened the door and pulled Zoey into a hug. Until that morning, Zoey had begun to like these spontaneous shows of affection. Deirdre and the Wilsons were clearly wearing her down. But now they felt even weirder than they had that first day. Now when she looked at Audra's mom, Zoey couldn't help feeling that the Wilsons had been keeping something from her. She knew that Audra's dad couldn't tell her about her mom's sessions, but he at least could have mentioned their connection. It seemed somehow creepy and dishonest.

You just have to give her the scholarship stuff and finish up in Audra's room, Zoey told herself. *That's all you've agreed to do.*

The smell of warm chocolate drifted past Zoey's nose. "I just pulled a pan of brownies out of the oven," Beverly said. "We can talk in the kitchen."

She led the way and Zoey sat down at the round table in the middle of the large, all-white kitchen. A tall glass of milk was waiting for her next to the heaping plate of brownies. *Hello, Betty Crocker.*

Beverly held the brownies out to Zoey with a big smile and Zoey helped herself to a large chocolaty square. Beverly sat down, propped her head on her hands, and watched Zoey eat, smiling. If it hadn't been so weird, it would have been sweet. "These were Audra's favorite," she confessed. "I knew you'd like them. And it's so nice to be able to make them for someone. . . ."

She drifted off and dabbed at her eyes but kept a smile glued to her face. Zoey took a sip of milk and swallowed. "They're delicious," she agreed, trying to keep things light. In truth, the first bite had been good, but the more Audra's mom talked, the more the brownies began to taste like chalk.

Beverly reached a hand across the table. "I know this has been hard for you, too," she said, softly giving Zoey's arm a pat. "It can't be easy to watch a friend die. Just know that whenever you're ready to talk about it, we're here."

Zoey nodded and quickly reached for another brownie. It was going to break Audra's mom when she found out Zoey and Audra were hardly friends, and how flipped out her daughter had been when she went over the edge of that bridge. Zoey just couldn't bring herself to tell her. And she didn't want to make up a lie — she respected the Wilsons too much for that. But they kept asking and asking.

Pushing the papers she'd gotten from the office at Stafford across the table, Zoey changed the subject. "I think setting up the scholarship fund will be pretty easy," she said. "You just need to name the fund and decide how you want the money to be spent. After that, it's as simple as making the initial contribution."

Beverly skimmed the papers. "I'll read these more carefully later," she said, getting to her feet and smoothing her A-line navy blue wool skirt. As usual, she was dressed in modern-cut, all-natural fabrics — and looked like an Eileen Fisher model. "I have a surprise for you . . . in Audra's room." She held out a hand.

Zoey felt a little ill as she got to her feet. When Beverly kept holding out her hand, Zoey took it hesitantly. Audra's mom grasped Zoey's fingers tightly as she led Zoey down the hall and up the stairs.

Glancing in the rooms as they passed them, Zoey admired the simple furnishings and clean lines. The Wilsons were all about modern efficiency. Nothing in the house was out of place. Audra's room was no different. Zoey heaved a sigh of relief. Audra's parents had obviously done quite a bit of work since Zoey had been there last week, because most of the things had been sorted through. Zoey spotted several large paper shopping bags sitting inside the open closet door. "Audra's clothes," Beverly explained. "I want you to have them."

Zoey was speechless — and totally creeped out. "You're so much like her!" Beverly sobbed, losing it. She dropped her head onto Zoey's shoulder and sniffed loudly. Audra's mom shuddered, and a fresh wave of tears spilled onto Zoey's black cashmere hoodie.

"You could have been sisters."

A sharp chill shot up Zoey's spine, and Alison's voice echoed in Zoey's head. *Do you think they're trying to turn you into her — I mean, make you their daughter?* She dropped Dr. Wilson's hand and ran.

Chapter Twenty-four

Across town, Kelly sat in a massage chair at her favorite salon, her feet relaxing in a bubbling mass of steamy water. She'd really been needing this pedicure — hadn't had one in almost two weeks. It felt great to relax while the hot water soothed her.

"You want *this* color?" Claudine, her regular pedicurist, looked at Kelly skeptically as she held up the bottle of Cranberry Bite lacquer.

Kelly looked up from *Vogue,* mildly irritated by the interruption. "That's what I gave you," she reminded the woman, raising her eyebrows. Then she softened. "I'm giving up Frostbite for Thanksgiving."

Claudine nodded before easing Kelly's feet out of the water and wrapping them in a fluffy white towel. Reclining in her chair, Kelly popped in her ear buds and dialed up a recent download on her pink iPod nano while Claudine attended her perfectly shaped and buffed toes.

As the music played, Kelly cheered inwardly about the upcoming holiday. Even her toes would be in the spirit! Personally, she could do without the formal dinner at her grandmother's house, but she only had one and a half days of school left before she got to take four and a half days off. And four and a half days of no school sounded like heaven.

Reaching into her white leather Dior handbag, Kelly grabbed her cell so she could make a quick call to her sweetie. But instead of her sleek Razr, she pulled out Dustin's old LG. Kelly turned the clunky phone over in her hands. Her curiosity was piqued. She knew it was wrong to look through his numbers, but whatever.

Kelly flipped open the phone and started to scroll while Claudine rubbed cuticle oil on her toes. She looked over Dustin's old text messages. There was some stuff about the real estate deal, a bunch of messages to some guy named Donnie asking for more time, whatever that meant, and a few calls and messages to Chad.

Suddenly Kelly spotted her name on the "sent" list. "That's weird," she murmured, opening one of the messages. She couldn't remember Dustin ever calling her. . . .

Kelly gasped. Sitting up straight, she snatched her feet out of Claudine's clutches, ruining her first coat of Cranberry Bite. The messages were from Truthteller!

"Miss Reeves!" Claudine complained, reaching for Kelly's foot.

Kelly set her feet back onto the towel-covered footrest. "Just take it off and start over," she said, distracted and thoroughly annoyed. Her toes were the least of her worries.

Kelly leaned back, steaming at Dustin. Who did he think she was? And did he really expect to get away with this?

"Think again, Dustin Simon," Kelly murmured. A slow smile spread across her face as she dropped the phone into the bubbling water at her feet. "And get ready for war."

Chapter Twenty-five

Tom drummed his fingers on the counter in the admin office while he waited for the secretary to give him the combination to Chad's locker. It was Wednesday morning, and he didn't want to be late for first period. Mrs. Naslund, his English Lit teacher, was a tardiness tyrant. But Chad had asked him to get his books and notebooks so he could start to catch up, and Tom wanted to take care of it before Thanksgiving break and before Chad had to start chemotherapy. Problem was, Chad couldn't remember the combination to his locker.

Finally, the secretary came back to the counter with three numbers written on a small piece of paper. "This is confidential, of course," she said, as if Chad had all kinds of stuff in his locker that people would want to get their hands on.

"Of course," Tom said, adopting his most serious and genuine "I understand completely" expression. He had a whole arsenal of expressions that adults liked to see. DA Daddy had trained him well.

Five minutes later, Tom was pulling open Chad's locker and shoving his books into a messenger bag. He didn't envy the task in front of Chad. His friend was seriously behind, and chemo was going to take a lot out of him. Not to mention the fact that he had no memory of the whole school year. All those facts and formulas and tables and novels . . . gone.

"Hey." A soft voice behind him made Tom spin around. Alison.

"Hey," Tom said back, feeling immediately foolish. Alison looked great dressed in a tight-fitting cotton blazer and was standing close enough for him to catch a whiff of whatever it was she wore that made him forget his name. The smell reminded him of all the afternoons they'd spent in room 308.

"Missed you at the hospital Saturday," she said softly.

Tom felt a rush of adrenaline. She missed him! "I've missed —"

"You helping Chad with his homework?" she asked, changing the subject and peering into the locker.

Tom nodded. He was helping, but not the way he used to. The days of giving Chad the answers were over. Just thinking about how much they'd cheated and how much it had hurt both of them made Tom feel awkward and ashamed. He used to think he was helping Chad, but if he had really wanted to help his friend he would have made Chad do the work himself. Tom stared at the bag full of books.

Alison shifted back and forth on her metallic flats. She seemed . . . anxious.

"You going to see him after school?" Tom asked, wishing he could say something to her that wasn't about Chad. Wishing he could say something about *them*. "He's going home today, I think."

Alison shook her head. "I'm not sure if he likes it when I visit," she confessed, looking up at Tom with her wide-set blue eyes.

"Sure he does," Tom said, surprised. "How could he not?"

Alison shrugged. "I don't know," she said. "It's just that the last time I was there . . ." She trailed off, rubbing her shoulder with her other hand. "Never mind," she said. She stood there still shifting back and forth, then smiled, but without her eyes. "Well, see ya." She gave Tom a small wave and started off down the hall.

"Yeah, see ya," Tom replied as he watched her walk away. He felt like kicking himself. Why was he always so freakin' brilliant when she was around? He needed a second take — a chance to say and do the *right* thing for once.

"She'll be okay," another, not-quite-so-familiar voice interrupted his thoughts. Tom whirled around to see X standing next to him, staring at him with those hypnotic eyes. How long had she been there?

"I know," Tom agreed, though he was comforted by the fact that X thought so. The girl had insight. "You're right." Tom nodded. *Alison* will *be okay. Actually, it's* me *I'm worried about.*

"And so will you," X added with a smile. Tom blinked in surprise. Had he said that out loud? X made him feel like an open book.

"Better than okay, even," X added before turning and walking down the hall in her mock school uniform.

"One can hope," Tom murmured after her long dark hair and retreating back. He turned back to Chad's locker and shrugged his shoulders, trying to shake off the feeling that X knew something he didn't.

Chapter Twenty-six

Chad struggled to open his eyes. They felt like they had been sealed shut with peanut butter. *I can't wake up,* he thought groggily. The idea made his pulse race and his eyes fly open. But the fluorescent lights made them close again just as quickly.

I can *wake up,* he reassured himself. He had not gone back into a coma, he was just coming around after being under anesthesia for yet another "procedure." The way the doctors and nurses called the minor operation to install his port-a-cath a procedure instead of an operation made Chad want to laugh. It was like they thought calling it something else made it easier.

But nothing took away the fact that they had to knock him out and cut him open.

Lifting the neck of his gown so he could see his chest, Chad dared to open his eyes again, this time just a crack. The port-a-cath was in. It was a simple white plastic disk pretty high on his chest with a gasket that opened into his bloodstream. Heidi told him it would make his chemo a lot easier — it was a straight shot for the anti-cancer chemicals and would keep him from getting multiple needle stab wounds every time he had to be injected. But the port looked weird and felt even weirder. It reminded Chad of the plastic thermometers that came in turkeys and popped up to tell you they were done cooking.

Oh, yeah, Thanksgiving. Chad let his eyes close and his head drop back on his pillow. He felt a little sick and thinking about plucked turkey was not helping. Thanksgiving was only a day away. He was going home. He should have been excited. But instead . . .

"Hey, you."

Kelly's voice was music to Chad's ears. He opened his eyes again, wide this time to drink in the sight of her. Standing next to his bed wearing a quilted corduroy coat, she was as gorgeous as ever. "Hi," Chad croaked. His voice was raspy.

"Here." Kelly turned to the wheeled table beside the bed and poured Chad water from the pink pitcher before hitting the button on the bed that brought him a little more upright.

"You poor thing," she murmured, handing him the cup before taking off her coat and hat and shaking her long hair so it fell down her back.

Chad accepted the plastic cup gratefully and took a sip. "How long have you been here?" he asked. "You should be home . . . with your family." For the first time Chad looked around the recovery room. There were two other patients lying in beds nearby, but no other visitors. Where were *his* parents? Probably at work.

"I'll have plenty of time to spend with family and the rest of Grandmother's guests tomorrow. Today I wanted to see you." Kelly pulled a chair close and sat down. "I wish we could spend the whole holiday together."

Smiling sleepily, Chad agreed. "Me too," he said, handing Kelly his cup. "Your Thanksgiving sounds like a lot more fun than mine."

"Fun? Oh, yes, dinner at Grandmother's house is always fun." Kelly's voice dripped sarcasm and she grinned wickedly. "Well, at least it's a spectacle. Her Highness always invites Silver Spring's flavor du jour. I'm sure Tom's family will be there — Tom's dad has a special place in his heart for Grandmother Diamond's checkbook, and of course she appreciates his political clout. Ew." Kelly screwed up her face. "I totally forgot that means Tom's evil twin, Zoey, will be there, too, this year. Hopefully she won't torch the joint. The Bourguets and the Longs usually show up to do some holiday kiss-up. And let's not forget Alison." Kelly pretended to gag. "She's *always* kissing up. Ugh, I hope she chokes on a bone."

Ignoring his own discomfort, Chad reached his hand toward Kelly. "Don't let her get to you," he said gently.

"Oh, don't worry about me. I'm tough," Kelly replied.

"I still wish I could be there." Chad squeezed Kelly's hand tighter, wishing he could tell her the other reason he wanted to be with her at the Diamond Estate: He did not want to be at his own house. In the past twenty-four hours he had recalled more and more about his home life. And the memories weren't all Hallmark moments. His parents fought constantly, it terrified Will, and Dustin only seemed to make things worse. The normal tension level at the Simon house made a guy feel like he was walking barefoot on broken glass.

"Maybe I could come over after the whole dead-bird ceremony is over," Kelly suggested. "We could curl up with some movies and popcorn and forget our families even exist." Her sea-green eyes sparkled, and Chad almost said yes without thinking. There was nothing Chad wanted more than to spend every waking second with Kelly. But he had another problem — his family secret. If Kelly came over, she would know in a second that the Simons were in a very different league than the Diamonds or Reeves. She wouldn't even have to see the peeling paint and the worn-out doormat to know that they would never be Tamara Diamond's flavor du jour.

"I wish you could." Chad pushed himself up a little higher on the bed. "But my mom's kind of a stickler about holidays and —"

Kelly held up a hand briefly before resting it on Chad's leg. "You don't have to tell me about moms and holidays. Hey, you're shaking. Are you cold?" Turning, Kelly waved down a nurse from the hallway. "He's shaking."

The nurse brought over a warm blanket and laid it over Chad, tucking it around his legs. "It's just the effect of the anesthesia. Lots of people get the shakes," she reassured Chad. "Let's ease you back down here. You'll be fine, you just have to take it easy."

Chad let the nurse adjust the bed so he was lying back down. He felt so stupid, lying around all the time. It made him anxious. But so did the thought of getting out of bed and going home.

I should be thankful, Chad chastised himself. Wasn't that what Thanksgiving was all about? *I'm awake. I'm alive. And I have Kelly.* Yes, Chad was thankful for at least two things: his best friend and his girlfriend. With them at his side, he could get through everything else.

"You'll be okay." Kelly scooted her chair so close it pressed right up against Chad's bed, then rested her head on his port-free shoulder. "I'll make sure of it."

"Thank you," Chad said. He ran his fingers through Kelly's hair. "Thanks for being here . . . and for staying with me." Kelly didn't say a word, but as Chad wrapped his arm around her he felt her relax into him.

He had everything he needed.

Chapter Twenty-seven

Standing in the massive foyer of her grand-mother's estate on Thanksgiving afternoon, Alison kissed the air on either side of Mrs. Long's face. "So nice to see you again," she lied. "You look fantastic," she lied again. She saw Dr. Long, his overly lifted wife, and their pompous twin sons about twice a year. And about once a year Mrs. Long cornered her and tried to get her to join the girls' auxiliary of the Junior League by telling her really long, really boring stories about all the fun they had organizing charity events. The only thing that got Alison through those conversations was wondering how Mrs. Long could talk with her skin pulled as tight as a trampoline.

Luckily for Alison, Mrs. Long did not linger in the grand entry hall. She ambled off on her husband's arm into the living room to devour hors d'oeuvres. Alison made a mental note to keep her distance.

Beside her, Alison's grandmother checked her diamond encrusted Cartier watch. Nearly all of the Thanksgiving guests had arrived. Alison would know, since she'd greeted every single one by her grandmother's side. It was Tamara's request that she play cohostess, and even though it was tedious to stand in the grand entry hall on three-inch shimmer suede Jimmy Choos and make small talk, a part of Alison was loving it. It seemed to signify that she was a real member of the household now, not just some charity case her grandmother had taken in. Plus, it was burning Kelly up.

Out of the corner of her eye Alison could see her cousin sitting on the settee in the living room with her arms and legs crossed, foot bouncing with annoyance, and trying not to look like she was watching every single thing that happened in the foyer. Smoothing her hands over her skirt, Alison was glad she had put on her Nicole Miller satin drop-waist. She knew the dress made her look older and more sophisticated, and Tamara had bought it for her preseason, so nobody else had it yet . . . not even Kelly.

Grandmother Diamond's butler was holding open the door for the last of the four invited families. As the Ramirez clan stepped in, Alison's welcoming smile was absolutely genuine for the first time all day.

"Zoey! You look fantastic!" Alison was wowed when Zoey shrugged off her coat and handed it to the butler. Alison hardly ever saw Zoey in a dress and the dark plum BCBG beaded number definitely worked for her. The two friends hugged while Tamara said her hellos to the DA and Deirdre.

"Is Tom here?" Alison asked, looking over Zoey's shoulder.

"Yeah, he's coming. He left something in the car." Alison followed Zoey's gaze as she took in the crowd in the living room and the explosion of autumn-hued flowers arranged on the mantel over the massive fireplace. A bar had been set up to one side and waiters in white tuxes and tails circulated with plates of tiny architectural appetizers.

"Some spread," Zoey whispered. Alison just raised her eyebrows. She'd forgotten this was Zoey's first real Diamond event. She hadn't bothered coming home from boarding school for many holidays. Her friend took a few steps toward the living room so she could get a closer look.

"Alison! You look so grown-up!" Deirdre grabbed Alison's hand, spinning her around. The perky blond was beaming as she leaned in to plant a real kiss on Alison's cheek. The first of the day.

"Thanks," Alison said. "And congratulations!" she added, remembering that Deirdre was pregnant.

"Shhh!" Deirdre dropped Alison's hand and held a long pink-painted nail in front of her lips and giggled. Her nail polish matched her lipstick perfectly. "It's still a secret. Dante doesn't want anyone to know yet. But isn't it wonderful?" she whispered loudly. With her other hand she cupped her still flat stomach and smiled down at it like she was already looking into the face of her newborn.

Even though she knew how much Zoey was opposed to the coming baby, Alison couldn't help but share Deirdre's excitement. Sure, she wasn't the brightest bulb, but her enthusiasm was genuine — and infectious. Alison put a finger to her own lips, assuring Deirdre she would keep quiet. But if Dierdre really wanted to keep her pregnancy a secret she should stop holding her stomach like the kid might spill out.

Turning to the DA, Alison held out a hand to welcome him and finish her greeting tour of duty. The stocky but imposing man ignored her completely.

"Alison, why don't you get our guests a refreshment? Dante and I have a little business to attend to," Grandmother Diamond said, slipping her hand around the DA's arm and letting him lead her to the library.

"Of course." Alison stepped back to allow Deirdre to follow Zoey into the living room.

"Ooh! I have to powder my nose first," Deirdre said, still clutching her stomach. The butler quickly stepped up to show Deirdre the way, and Alison grabbed Zoey's hand.

"Looks like you're my date now," she said, making her way toward the bar. "Two Pom spritzers," she ordered. Then, turning back to Zoey, she asked, "So what do you think?"

"I'll tell you in a sec," Zoey replied, grabbing a paper-thin potato crisp decorated with crème fraiche, caviar, and a chive spear from a passing tray and popping it in her mouth. "Tasteful," she said, chewing and wiping Deirdre's pink lipstick off Alison's cheek with her cocktail napkin at the same time.

Alison led Zoey over to two chairs in the corner. It was the perfect spot to take it all in. And it was behind Kelly, who was trying to escape her mother, Phoebe. They could see everything without catching her evil eye.

The more than a dozen guests were happily chatting away. Alison thought she noticed some of them glancing toward the entry waiting for their hostess to come in. But mostly the Bourguets were happy to talk yachts with the Longs, who were happy to hear Hollywood stories from Aunt Christine, who was happy to talk about herself. And the icky Long twins were happy to leer at Kelly. Gross.

"So do you guys do this every Thanksgiving?" Zoey asked, grabbing a petite souffle from the next offered tray.

"Grandmother always does *something*. But in years past I've always kind of been stuck between two houses." Alison took a sip of her drink, remembering last year. Her mom had been in a frenzy. She was going all out and had her hands in every literal and figurative pie. The Rose family Thanksgiving was not just a family event, it was all about Looking Good. Of course the staff and cameras had been there to record every succulent moment for a future magazine article. Her mom had been so concerned with how everything looked, she forgot to keep Alison's dad on a short leash.

"As soon as Dad passed out in the cranberry mold I'd usually come here," Alison tried to joke, but Zoey saw through it and gave her a sympathetic smile.

"Seriously, you should have seen my mom last year," Alison said in a low voice. "The veins in her neck were popping out so hard I thought her head might explode. After she called off the camera crews and told the guests Dad had the flu, she sent me over here.

"I *know* it's bad when Mom sends me to enemy territory. She stayed cool in front of everyone, but I think when she was finally alone she probably had a screaming fit and took a baseball bat to the turkey."

"I wish the camera crews had caught that." Zoey laughed.

Alison forced a laugh, too. Picturing her mom actually losing control was hard to imagine. With a wave of guilt, she wondered how her mother was spending this Thanksgiving. She doubted Helen Rose was feeling very thankful.

At that moment Alison noticed her grandmother and the DA rejoining the party. Before Tamara was all the way in the room, one of the white-clad waitstaff was serving her and the DA their drinks. Gin and tonic for

Grandmother, something brown with two cubes of ice for the DA.

Catching Alison's eye, Tamara raised her glass. Alison held up her own and smiled.

Maybe, Alison thought, *this is where I've belonged all along.*

Chapter Twenty-eight

Holding on to the wooden handrail, Chad walked carefully down the stairs. When the anesthesia had worn off yesterday in the hospital, he'd started to feel a little like his old self. But after today's ride home and the exhausting welcome, he could feel just how atrophied his muscles had become. There was no denying he was weak — and when the chemo started he was probably going to get weaker.

But at least I'm out of the hospital.

"Hey, Mom, what's for dinner?" Chad asked when he finally reached the ground floor. He stepped into the kitchen and was bombarded by Thanksgiving chaos. The smell of turkey was almost overwhelming and every counter was cluttered with ingredients and dirty dishes.

"Oh, you." Chad's mom flapped a floured hand at him before going back to rolling out dough. "Why don't you go see if your dad needs any help with the table?"

In the dining room Chad's dad was smoothing the good, cream-colored tablecloth over the table. Chad watched his father's large hands pass over the red wine stain on one of the corners and smiled. He remembered that stain! He even remembered the way his mom had yelled when Will had tipped over her glass. His memory seemed to be coming back in small chunks.

Will was standing at the credenza counting out silverware. His lips were moving, but he was not talking.

"Need some help?" Chad asked. Will shook his head no.

Chad's dad tossed him some napkins. "You can set these out."

Laying a napkin at each place at the table, Chad noted there were only four. Dustin would not be joining them. Behind him, Will circled the table placing the silverware — a perfect job for him since he liked everything just so. No utensils were allowed to touch and the knife blades *had* to be facing in.

Suddenly the doorbell rang, making Chad jump. Hope and fear fluttered in his chest. Maybe Kelly was done with her holiday duty and had come to see him after all.

"I'll get it," he said quickly. But as he walked to open the door he realized he was being ridiculous. No way was Kelly at his door. First, he'd told her not to come. Second, she probably hadn't even eaten yet.

You don't really want her at the door, anyway, Chad reminded himself. The more Chad remembered, the more keeping his family situation a secret made sense to him.

Chad pulled open the door. "Dustin! What are you doing here?"

"Hey, bro," Dustin said quietly, looking over Chad's shoulder to see if he was alone. "I was hoping it would be you."

Chad squinted at his older brother. "You were?"

"Yeah. I, uh, lost my cell phone. I thought maybe I left it at the hospital."

"Nope. Sorry," Chad said, shaking his head. His plastic bag of patient belongings did not include his brother's phone, just some dirty clothes and his watch.

"Well, what I really need is your girlfriend's phone number. You don't remember it, do you?" Dustin asked, looking a little sheepish.

Chad shook his head. Was Dustin joking? He was busy remembering who he was. Digits hadn't even entered into his mind yet.

"Dustin, is that you?" Mr. Simon stepped into the hall behind Chad and opened the door wider.

"Uh, hi, Dad." Dustin scraped the bottom of his boot on the edge of the concrete steps, knocking off some flecks of peeling paint.

There was an awkward silence before Chad's dad spoke again. "Why don't you come in?"

Dustin hesitated.

"Chad, who is it?" his mom called, stepping into the hall and wiping her hands on a dish-towel. Chad watched her carefully, not sure what her reaction to her oldest son would be. He had noticed that his parents and big brother were almost never at the hospital at the same time, and if they were they talked to him, not to each other.

Staring at Dustin, Chad's mom looked stunned. She bit her lips together for a long second. "Won't you stay for dinner?" she asked. Her words were plain and direct, but her eyes were practically begging.

Dustin must have seen the pleading look, too, because he took a big step inside and closed the door. "Thanks, Mom. That would be great."

"Let me take your coat."

"Are you thirsty?"

Suddenly Chad's parents were all over Dustin like he was the one who had kicked *them* out. "Nah, I'm fine. Really. I can get something if I need it."

Chad's mom dabbed at her eyes with the corner of her towel. Then she gave up trying to keep it all in. "It's so good to be all together again!" she sobbed, throwing her arms around her oldest son. "My boys are back."

"Boys are back. Boys are back," Will echoed, wandering into the hall. He was rocking back and forth on his feet, going from one foot to the other. Emotional displays sometimes set him off. But Chad recognized the slightly uncomfortable look on his face as a smile. "Good to be together." He nodded.

"The turkey is almost done," Chad's mom sniffed, pulling herself away from Dustin and doing one last eye dab.

"And we have another place to set." Chad's dad tried to direct Will back out toward the dining room.

"The salad fork goes on the outside," Will informed them all before launching into an avalanche of holiday information in monotone. "Thanksgiving is for Pilgrims. The first Pilgrims landed in Plymouth. That's in Massachusetts. You can get there on the bus. Take the Massachusetts Express." He nodded. "Greyhound Mass. Express. Go Greyhound," Will insisted before he left Chad alone with Dustin in the hall.

"Family time just like you remember it?" Dustin asked, grinning at Chad.

"Pretty much," Chad said, smiling back. Better, actually. Most of the family moments he remembered were fights. Was this time together a fluke? Or was it possible he just didn't remember the happier moments . . . yet?

Throwing an arm over Chad's shoulder, Dustin pulled him closer. "So, don't you have a cell phone somewhere?" he asked. Chad squirmed uncomfortably out of his brother's grasp. His family was getting along fine, but suddenly Chad wondered why Dustin had shown up at the door.

Chapter Twenty-nine

It's like dinner and a movie, Zoey thought, relaxing into the high-backed chair in the corner of the Diamond living room. She drank in the scene while she sipped her spritzer.

A fire crackled in the huge marble fireplace, and standing in front of it Alison's aunt Christine was entertaining Silver Spring's most pompous blue-blood, Harding Cross, and his third wife, Lula. Zoey adjusted herself in the chair so she could watch Christine work. Even though Zoey couldn't hear what the actress was saying, the statuesque blond's body language told her all she needed to know. Christine was leaning in flirtatiously, gesturing with her hands and sharing knowing looks with Harding. Mr. Cross could not take his eyes off the actress, while his wife glared and sipped her wine so ferociously Zoey thought she might take a bite out of the stemmed crystal.

As Zoey continued to watch, Christine drew Kelly's dad, Bill, into the conversation. Next she hooked the DA and Deirdre. The bigger her audience, the happier she appeared. And her monologue just got louder and louder. Watching her, Zoey found it hard to believe that it had ever been a secret that Christine was Kelly's biological mom. It just seemed obvious.

Growing bored with the show, Zoey stood up to look for Alison. Her grandmother had asked her to do something, and she said she'd be right back. But she wasn't. Tom was still MIA, too. Maybe the two of them were hiding out somewhere together.

Zoey was headed for the hall when a slender hand on her shoulder held her back. "Zoey."

Turning, Zoey's heart revved. "Oh, Mrs. Diamond." She had been around Alison's grandmother quite a bit lately, but the woman still made her nervous. "I was looking for Alison," Zoey blurted.

"She'll be right back," Tamara said, blinking slowly. "I was hoping to get a chance to chat with you." Mrs. Diamond's thin hand snaked its way around Zoey's bare arm and she led Zoey to the settee.

"Of course." Zoey could not get away. "It was so nice of you to invite us."

"What's this I hear about you helping set up a scholarship fund for the Wilson girl?" Tamara asked, sitting down and patting the seat beside her.

Zoey sat as far away as she dared. "Um . . ." She was not sure what to say. She was surprised Tamara knew anything about it. Surely Alison hadn't told her.

"The Wilsons want to honor the memory of their daughter in some concrete way," Zoey explained. When she spoke she could almost hear Beverly saying those exact words. And thinking of the Wilsons in their quiet house — their first holiday without their only daughter — made Zoey feel a little sad. She shouldn't have run off so abruptly the last time she'd been there. "I'm just helping with some of the paperwork. That's all," she finished.

"What?" *Of course* Kelly had to walk by at that moment and listen in on the conversation. And the look in her snakey green eyes was pure amusement. "*You* are helping set up a scholarship to honor *Audra*? That is so rich!" Kelly laughed sharply. "I guess a little guilt goes a long way."

"Kelly, that will be enough," Tamara cut her off, but Zoey didn't think she looked entirely displeased with her granddaughter's mocking tone. Kelly wasn't chastened, either. She grinned wickedly at Zoey before scanning the room for someone to share her latest joke with.

Ugh. Where was Alison? Things were going downhill fast.

As if on cue, Alison appeared in the doorway and gave her grandmother a small nod. Tamara excused herself and stood in the center of the room. She made a tiny coughing noise and all conversation ceased. Smiling benevolently, the hostess spoke. "I'm so happy you could join us on this special day. Alison has just informed me that our meal is ready to be served. Please follow me to the dining room." Tamara turned, holding her arm out to Alison, who hurried over to take it.

The rest of the guests moved slowly through the arched living room entry. Zoey found herself walking right next to Kelly and prayed she wouldn't have to sit by her, too.

"Did you bring your matches, Ramirez?" Kelly said quietly, so only Zoey could hear it. She was smiling and looking straight ahead.

"Why are you even talking to me?" Zoey hissed back, plastering on her own fake smile when she noticed her dad looking. "Don't you have some ransom you should be paying?"

"You're off the hook this time," Kelly snarled through her smile. "But you are not off my radar, so watch your step."

Zoey did not notice Kelly's foot until she was stumbling into Mrs. Long's back.

"Oh!" the surgically enhanced woman cried when she felt the unexpected touch.

"So sorry!" Zoey apologized, struggling to regain her footing. "My, uh, my shoe got caught on the carpet."

"Our apologies, Mrs. Long." Out of nowhere Dante Ramirez had swooped in to make sure Zoey's humiliation was complete. "Zoey, you need to be more careful."

Thanks, Dad. Ignoring her father and the screecher, Zoey locked eyes with Kelly. "Don't worry," she said in a threatening voice, "it won't happen again."

Chapter Thirty

Standing behind her chair in the dining room, Alison tried to see what was going on in the hall. It wasn't easy. A large floral arrangement was blocking her view and the guests were all milling about looking for their names.

As the scuffle broke up and the rest of the guests came in, Alison spotted Kelly. She looked pinched. Zoey was right near her and looked furious.

Glancing at her grandmother, Alison did not dare leave her post. She and Zoey had barely had a chance to talk and now it looked like she was going to be seated halfway across the room!

Alison had made several covert attempts to sneak into the dining room to rearrange the seating place cards, to no avail. Her grandmother had kept her busy with a long list of tasks.

So her folded place card remained next to her grandmother's at the head of the long table while Zoey's was all the way at the other end hidden behind several giant centerpieces.

Kelly, Aunt Phoebe, and Uncle Bill were near the center, across from Harding and Lula Cross. Craning her neck, Alison saw that Tom had finally shown up. He was next to Zoey at the end of the table, near the Bourgets, and keeping his head down. And here at the head of the table . . . Alison looked at the place card *next* to hers. Oh, no.

"Oh, goody! Now we can finally talk!" Mrs. Long pulled out the chair beside Alison's and planted her bony butt in it. "The Junior League is working on several exciting new youth projects," she crowed. "I've been meaning to call you to pick your little brain. And now we can talk in person! I think that's so much better, don't you?"

"Much better." Alison faked a smile for her grandmother's benefit and sat down with a sigh. Things could be worse. At least she wasn't next to Kelly, and she was at her grandmother's side. It was a place of honor and she had earned it.

Across the table Aunt Christine found her name and sat down, another stroke of luck for Alison. In less than two seconds Christine and Mrs. Long were off on a new topic — the latest Botox cocktails — and Alison was off the hook. Spreading her white linen napkin in her lap, Alison felt truly thankful. Things had been hard for a long time, but she was actually starting to feel okay about her place in the family. The Diamonds were not conventional — far from it. But they were strong and powerful. Alison looked at her aunts in turn. Aunt Phoebe had testified against Alison's mother. At the time, Alison had been horrified, but now she under-stood. She, like Alison, was doing what she had to do. And all of them would be rewarded by the family ruler.

Alison watched her grandmother silently survey the room from her place in the center of it all. When her gaze met Alison's, she smiled tightly. Alison smiled back.

At last everyone was in his or her place. Beside Aunt Christine only one empty seat remained. Alison wondered if her aunt had a date that hadn't shown and was momentarily embarrassed for her.

Then Tamara stood to make a toast and silenced a room for the second time that day.

"Thank you all for coming. This is a day to show our gratitude and I know my family in particular has much to be grateful for. This year has not been easy." Grandmother smiled at her understatement. "But, in the Diamond tradition, we've stuck together and have come out of it unscathed."

Alison held her head up, aware some eyes were on her. "Unscathed" and "together" was probably not how she would have put it. And it was not like her grandmother to talk about family matters in public.

"Now at last things are falling into place. And at last our dear Alison has a real family to raise her again."

Alison let the glass she had been holding at

the ready sink back to the table, where it hit her knife with a small clink. Where was this going?

"A child needs a mother and a father, and though I have done my best during these trying times, I know I am not enough for my granddaughter."

What is she talking about? Alison wondered as panic began to rise.

"That is why I am delighted that my dear daughter Phoebe and her husband, Bill, have agreed to take Alison home to live with them and raise her as their own alongside their daughter, Kelly."

Every drop of blood drained from Alison's face.

Far down the table Kelly dropped her glass. Alison heard it shatter — like her life — into tiny pieces.

And then from the other side of the flowers came a retching noise that made Alison tilt her head in time to see Deirdre bend over and barf into her pink Chanel purse.

Chapter Thirty-one

"Get rid of it." Zoey's dad clamped Deirdre's barf-filled bag shut and handed it under the table to Zoey.

"Me?" Zoey looked at her dad with disbelief. The last thing she wanted to deal with was a puke-filled purse. Her best friend had just had the rug pulled out from under her! Zoey needed to stay put in case Alison needed her — and so she could find out what would happen next.

"Yes, you," DA Ramirez said, barely moving his lips. He was talking so low he was practically growling. "Haven't I cleaned up plenty of your little messes?"

"Fine." Zoey rolled her eyes at her brother, who gave her a helpless look. Then she grasped the bag, trying to ignore the repulsive fact that it was warm, and headed out of the dining room the same way her pregnant stepmother and a furious Kelly (followed closely by her mom Phoebe) had gone a moment before.

Moving quickly and holding the purse away from her body, Zoey snuck a look back at her best friend. The poor girl looked like a ghost. The expression on Alison's face made Zoey's stomach knots tie themselves even tighter. *Oh, Al!*

Alison's eyes shifted, meeting Zoey's gaze. Zoey tried hard to silently convey how sorry she was. She wished that she were dragging Alison out of the airless room instead of . . . ew. The rank liquid in the bag was starting to leak through the lining. She needed to ditch Deirdre's bag, now.

Standing in the three-story foyer, Zoey was not sure where to go next. The nearest bathroom was already taken — she could hear Deirdre losing the rest of her appetizers inside. And down the hall to the right she could hear Kelly screaming and Phoebe shushing.

"How could you do this without even telling me?" Kelly's voice was growing fainter. Her mom must be taking her to another wing to throw her hissy fit in private. Zoey smirked. At least the unpleasant new living arrangement was a blow to Kelly, too.

It was tempting to follow the disappearing voices and listen in — but then there was the bag.

Zoey took the back way to the large Diamond kitchen. It was, of course, filled with waitstaff ready to serve the plated turkey dinner.

"In here." Francesca, the cook, took in the situation at once and held out a large trash bag. Zoey dropped in the purse. Chucking the bag entirely might not have been what DA Daddy'd had in mind, but there was no way Zoey was cleaning everything out. And she couldn't well force one of the servants to do it — that would be so wrong. Barfo-mama would just have to buy a new one.

"Thanks." Zoey breathed through her nose again when the trash bag was tied shut and the lethal scent was contained. Francesca nodded like she was used to this kind of stuff and went back to her work.

After washing her hands, Zoey hurried back to the dining room to check on Alison.

Her best friend was still sitting like a stone, unmoving. She was not screaming or crying or even pouting, she was practically expression-less, which was even worse. She looked like the slightest bump would tip her over and she would shatter like an icicle. Zoey wished she could go to her, but beside her Tamara Diamond looked formidable.

"Can you believe this?" Zoey whispered to Tom as she slipped into her seat. Deirdre was not back yet and two white-coated waiters were just finishing cleaning up the glass at Kelly's place.

"What?" Tom looked like he had just walked in.

"Alison going to live with Kelly!" Zoey whis-pered, exasperated. "Talk about thrown to the wolves." She almost regretted what she said. Tom and Kelly used to be friends — or rather, Tom used to carry an Olympic-sized torch for her.

Tom just nodded, looking completely dis-tracted. Maybe he was thinking about how bad it would be for Alison. He had not stopped star-ing at her through the flower arrangement.

"Forget it." Zoey gave up. She didn't really want to talk to Tom about this, anyway. She wanted to talk to Alison. Placing her napkin next to her plate, she started to get up again and head for a bathroom. She hoped that Alison would get the hint and follow her out. But then something made Zoey sit back down.

"No way." Just when it seemed like things could not get any weirder . . . the butler entered, followed by a young man in a suit and tie.

"What is *he* doing here?" Tom whispered.

Zoey stared at Jeremy. She had no idea.

Chapter Thirty-two

"Jeremy!" Alison watched Aunt Christine pop up like a jack-in-the-box and wave at Zoey's tutor, who had just been shown in. She felt like she was watching the whole scene from underwater. Nothing was making any sense.

Jeremy smiled and made his way to the head of the table. Christine put her hand on the chair next to hers. The empty seat mystery was solved. But how in the world did Jeremy know Aunt Christine? Alison seriously hoped they weren't dating.

"I'm so glad you could make it," Christine gushed. "I just couldn't bear the thought of you being alone. Holidays are for friends and family."

So they can reach you easier with their knives, Alison thought, not daring to look at her grandmother. She had not looked at her since she finished her little speech. In fact, she had not opened her mouth.

"You know, you're a lot like our Alison," Christine said, motioning across the table. "She's separated from her parents this year, too."

"Nice to see you." Jeremy nodded at Alison and kissed Christine on both cheeks. Then he stepped around Christine and offered a hand to Grandmother Diamond. "I'm so sorry I'm late."

Tamara ignored the offered hand. Undeterred, Jeremy brought his other hand from behind his back. He was holding a small wrapped bouquet. Alison watched her grandmother take it without a word and glance at the flowers before handing them off to a servant. Alison smelled the delicate and unmistakable scent of lily of the valley — her grandmother's favorite flower. They were not easy to get in November — Jeremy must have known somehow that Grandmother Diamond loved them.

"I was delighted when Christine invited me and truly appreciate your hospitality," Jeremy went on. He offered his hand again and this time Alison's grandmother took it.

"Mother, this is Jeremy Jones," Christine purred. Alison saw a look of disappointment on Christine's face when Tamara did not react. "As in Harris Jones," she added.

Alison sucked in her breath. Did she hear that right? Jeremy was related to Harris Jones, *the* Harris Jones — the movie mogul?

"Don't be gauche," Grandmother Diamond reprimanded Christine. "Name dropping is unattractive." Turning back to Jeremy and removing her hand from his, she added, "Of course I know who your father is. In fact, I know who you are as well. Please, have a seat."

Jeremy sat. Alison thought he looked a little shocked and pleased to hear Tamara Diamond knew who he was, but he didn't say anything.

"What I don't know is how you knew my favorite flower, or how you became acquainted with my daughter Christine." Grandmother Diamond sat back so that the servers could place her plate in front of her. "So you and I clearly have quite a bit to talk about." She smiled tightly before picking up her fork and knife.

Risking a lecture about staying in her seat, Alison leaned around the centerpiece to see if Zoey was getting all of this. Her friend's dark eyes were as big as dinner plates. Apparently the Harris Jones thing was news to her, too. Harris Jones was news no matter how or when he came up. For years he had commanded the box office as a heartbreaking leading man. After he was big enough to do any movie he wanted, he branched into directing. He got the films that "mattered" made, and with his name attached to them, they became blockbusters, too. He was big-time. Christine had been lucky to have a supporting role in his latest epic and was obviously doing what she could to make sure their collaboration continued.

"This looks delicious," Jeremy said politely before sampling his turkey. "Aren't you going to try it?" he asked, turning toward Alison.

Picking up her fork, she played with her mashed potatoes and watched Jeremy dig in. She thought she saw him trying to catch Zoey's eye, probably to apologize for the weird way she found out about his family.

Zoey was definitely going to be mad. It was terrible being the last to know — and Zoey told Jeremy *everything*. But Alison could relate to Jeremy keeping his dad under wraps, too. People acted weird when they got close to fame. They started to treat you differently.

Making little swirls in her gravy, Alison considered this news about Jeremy. She remembered he'd once mentioned something about his mom giving him his Saab to make up for time not spent together. That meant Jeremy had a celebrity dad and an absentee mom. With her own famous mom and disappearing dad, Alison could totally relate. They were both virtually parentless. But, Alison seethed as her anger at her grandmother flared; they were not orphans to be given away.

Suddenly Alison felt ill. Her grandmother had taken her in and cared for her with only one goal in mind: to get her own daughter convicted. Now that Alison had done what she'd wanted, she was tossing her away. It was disgusting — and not surprising in the least. Yet Alison hadn't been expecting it. Once again Alison had played the fool.

A buzzing in her clutch sent Alison fumbling for her phone under the table. Cell phones were not allowed in Grandmother Diamond's presence, and taking one out at the table — even just to look at it — was unthinkable. But Alison had hers set to vibrate, so nobody could hear it over the chatter, and at this moment she didn't really care what her grandmother's rules were. Following them clearly hadn't gained her anything. Peeking discreetly at the lit-up screen under the table, Alison's pulse quickened.

"Excuse me," she mumbled. Standing abruptly, she dropped her napkin in her chair. With her phone hidden in the palm of her hand, she hurried out of the room to take the call.

Chapter Thirty-three

"She can NOT live at our house!" Kelly screamed at her mother, who cringed and put her hand to her own lips. As if that would quiet Kelly down. "I don't care who hears me. You can't do this to me. You can't!" Kelly was screaming so loudly her throat ached. She welcomed the pain and wished her grandmother's precious guests could hear her. But her mom had whisked her away to one of the outer wings of the enormous house. There were two stories and a dozen walls between Kelly and the Tamara Diamond fan club meeting.

"Are you even listening?" Kelly shouted again at her mother, who was just standing there cringing. Desperate for a reaction, Kelly grabbed an intricate Limoges elephant from the collection on the table in the guest suite and held it over her head, threatening to smash it. But it was just for show. She wanted her mother to be as outraged as she felt — after all, she had apparently invited the enemy to live in their home.

"No!" Phoebe scrambled to retrieve the expensive bauble.

"Fine," Kelly said, letting it drop into her mother's hands.

"Oh, honey, I know you're upset," Phoebe crooned, putting the jeweled elephant safely back on its feet and placing herself between the pricey collectibles and Kelly. "But think of how poor Alison must feel. Her mother is in prison and her father is dealing with his . . . issues." Her mom dropped her voice.

"So what?" Kelly screamed. "*I* didn't make Aunt Helen break the law. *I* didn't make Uncle Jack drink. Why should *I* suffer for their mistakes?"

"Sweetie, please listen. I need you to be generous." Her mom reached out to touch Kelly's hand, but she spun away from her.

"It's just not fair," Kelly fumed. She was whining, Kelly knew, but sometimes that worked best on her mom. Sinking onto the bed, she let her hand fall in her lap. She could not remember the last time she'd felt so rattled.

"Alison needs our help," Kelly's mom knelt in front of her and tried to look up into her eyes. She was pleading. "The poor thing just lost her mother. It's our duty as family to make sure she's looked after. Your grandmother can't do it anymore, and it's the least we can do for her, considering how much she gives us."

Kelly crossed her arms over her chest and looked away. She wasn't buying any of the "duty" stuff. Her mom was clearly just echoing back the same lines Grandmother Diamond had used to convince her to take Alison in. But Kelly knew this move had nothing to do with duty and everything to do with being in Tamara's good graces. It was about scoring brownie points — and securing a larger inheritance. "This is about 'the list,' isn't it?" she said cruelly. "This is about how big a piece of the Diamond pie Grandmother leaves you."

"No!" her mom practically shouted. She probably wanted to believe that she was just a good mother hen clucking over little Orphan Ali and not a greedy pig like everyone else in the family. Except that she was as greedy as they came.

And when Kelly looked her in the eye, she saw that they both knew the truth. "So now you'll be raising both of your sisters' unwanted daughters, huh?" Kelly said.

Her mother's face fell. "I always wanted you," she whispered, her eyes tearing up.

"Yeah. You have such a big heart. . . ." Kelly said icily. "Or is that your wallet?"

If she heard, Kelly's mom pretended not to notice. She was standing up and brushing invisible lint off her skirt and preparing to brush the rest of the mess under the carpet. "We have so much to give, Kelly," Phoebe sighed. "And Alison needs us." She held her hands out and Kelly let her mom pull her off the bed and over to the art deco vanity with its huge round mirror. Side by side they fixed their hair and checked their makeup.

Alison needs us, Kelly repeated in her head, turning to catch her profile. *And I will give her plenty.*

Kelly smoothed her hair and thought about the saying Grandmother Diamond had taught her. "Keep your friends close and your enemies closer." Kelly would keep Alison close, all right.

Following her mother back down to the dining room, Kelly scanned the table. Alison was not in her seat. And across from her empty chair there was a newcomer — Zoey's college hottie.

The dimpled guy was sitting beside Aunt Christine and apparently charming that bore Mrs. Long. The woman's expression hadn't changed — it could no longer be altered without a scalpel. But the hoots coming out of her tight lips had to be laughter.

Kelly walked straight over and waited to be noticed.

"Oh, Kelly. You're back." Aunt Christine turned in her chair. "Jeremy, I'd like you to meet my niece Kelly."

Jeremy smiled and offered his hand. Kelly took it and held on. "Haven't we met before?" Kelly asked coyly. "You look so familiar."

Out of the corner of her eye, Kelly saw Zoey staring daggers. *Get an eyeful.*

"I'm not sure we've been officially introduced," Jeremy said. His eyes were sparkling — and it wasn't just the candlelight. "Jeremy Jones."

"I'm Kelly Reeves. Nice to meet you officially, Jeremy." Kelly leaned in and kissed him on the cheek. *Very nice indeed.*

Chapter Thirty-four

"Daddy?" Even locked behind the heavy bath-room door Alison did not dare raise her voice above a whisper. She had not talked to her father since he had disappeared a month before. And if her grandmother knew he was calling . . . Well, she had already ripped everything from Alison today.

"Daddy, is that you?" The phone crackled and made a weird metallic noise.

Then her father's deep voice came over the line. "Hi, angel. Happy Thanksgiving."

Just hearing the familiar voice choked Alison up, and she struggled to hold it together. So many questions were popping into her head, she didn't know what to ask first. And along with the questions was a golden flicker of hope. Maybe her dad had called because he was coming home . . . she wouldn't have to live with Kelly! "Daddy, are you coming home?" Alison choked out. She could barely breathe as she waited for his answer. Maybe he was already back in the country, already out of rehab.

"I wish I were, Alison. I really do. But . . ." He drifted off, and Alison's heart lurched. His voice sounded strained. Something was not right.

"What is it?" Alison did not bother to hide the panic in her voice. "What's wrong?"

"It's okay," her dad tried to calm her down. "Your grandmother's lawyers are here, that's all. And they want me to sign some papers."

That's all? "What papers?"

"They are asking me to give up my parental rights as long as I'm in rehab." There was silence on both ends for several seconds. Alison felt the last tiny shreds of control over her own life slipping out of her grasp.

"It's just temporary, I promise. Al, are you there? Are you okay?"

No! Alison wanted to scream. *I am not okay. I need you here now!* "Yes, I'm still here," was all she said.

"Look, if I don't sign they will take me to court and have me declared unfit. If they do that, I could lose you forever. These guys mean business."

Alison slumped down on the toilet seat. She did not want to be able to see her face in the mirror when she started to cry. She hated the ugly way her mouth screwed up, and the tears were definitely coming. "Dad, please don't let her do this. She's sending me to live with Kelly and —"

"Phoebe and Bill will take good care of you. And don't worry. We'll fight this."

"Okay," Alison said. But she knew it was hopeless. She'd just witnessed what happened when you tried to fight Tamara Diamond. Alison's mother was one of the strongest people she knew, and her grandmother had taken her down with barely a struggle — thanks to Alison. Alison had *never* seen her grandmother lose at anything.

"I just have to get better first, so I can prove I'm fit. We can't take any chances. I'm not going to let anyone take you away from me." Alison wanted to believe him but couldn't.

"I love you, Alison. I need you to know that. I may only have another minute to talk, and there are some things I need to tell you — things I can't put in a letter. You still have the key, right?"

Jack Rose's voice dropped lower as he spoke and it sounded muffled, too. He probably had his hand cupped around the receiver and his mouth. Alison pressed her cell phone to her ear, struggling to hear him. The volume was already as high as it could go. "Wait. Dad, I have to tell you something, too. Mom got convicted . . . and it's all my fault. I could have helped her — but I didn't."

When the words were out of her mouth Alison felt her stomach clench. She had finally spoken the truth aloud. She — not her grandmother — was the one to blame for her fractured family. She had put her mom in prison. It was all her fault.

"Daddy?" she breathed, waiting for his reaction. There was no response.

"Daddy!" Alison yelled. Her voice echoed off the Italian-tiled bathroom walls. It was too late. The line was dead.

Chapter Thirty-five

Shifting his weight from one foot to the other, Tom waited impatiently at one end of the cavernous foyer of the Diamond Estate for the door to the hall bathroom to open. Behind him, in the dining room, most of the Thanksgiving guests were politely enjoying their gourmet turkey meal and saving just enough room for the pumpkin chiffon and pecan pies to come. But Tom could not eat. All he could think about was Alison — and the moment he had been putting off for too long.

It had been difficult to come today, and even harder to come inside. He had been alternately desperate and afraid to see Alison. What if she didn't want to hear what he had to say? What if she didn't feel the same way?

Tom was kicking himself for spending so long sitting outside in the car, listening to music and mustering up his courage. He had blown so many chances already. By the time he came in, it was time to be seated — and then Mrs. Diamond announced Alison was moving in with Kelly, and then Zoey's tutor showed up. He had almost given up hope of talking to Alison alone when he saw her bolt out of the dining room by herself. He had followed in time to see her close herself in the downstairs bath closest in the foyer. And now here he was standing outside the door wondering if she would ever come out.

Yeah, this won't be awkward or anything. Tom shook his head. *Girls love it when you stalk them outside the bathroom.* But he couldn't give up — he had to tell her.

When the handle finally turned, Tom cleared his throat. It was now or never. The door swung slowly open and Alison emerged. She startled when she saw him, and their eyes locked.

Tom cleared his throat again. Alison looked so beautiful. Then he noticed her eyes were glistening. There was no smile on her lips, and her face was flushed. Tom felt like he had come upon a deer in the woods.

Don't run away, Tom thought. Though he wasn't sure if the thought was for Alison or himself.

"Alison, I . . ." Tom forced himself to speak, hoping he would say the right thing. But before he could get three words out, Alison's eyes filled with tears.

"I've been thinking about you a lot," he managed. That sounded lame. But it was true. He'd been thinking of her — and the time they spent together in the hospital — constantly. He had been missing her, too, like crazy. She'd helped him so much when he was really hurting about Chad and Audra, and now *she* was hurting.

Tom took a step forward. "I miss you," he said softly, hoping it would melt away the look of pain in Alison's blue eyes. It didn't.

What are you doing? Tom scolded himself. Now he sounded like he needed her when he was trying to be there *for* her. "You know all the time we spent together . . . I . . . Well, I really like you, and —"

Alison was shaking her head. Tom was not sure if the look on her face was surprise or horror.

Then a tear slid down one of Alison's cheeks. She brushed it away angrily.

It was horror. Definitely horror. "Tom . . . I . . . I . . ." *She doesn't even know what to say.*

And neither did he.

"I'm sorry," Alison whispered hoarsely. She pushed past Tom and ran up the huge staircase, away from the party, away from him.

Nice. Tom let out a ragged breath as he watched her go. When he heard a door slam, he squeezed his eyes shut, trying to block out what an idiot he had been.

You blew it. Again.

Chapter Thirty-six

After the call from her dad and her awful exchange with Tom, Alison did not return to the table. She felt terrible about running away from Tom like that, but she couldn't have that conversation. Not then.

Alone in her room, Alison knew she couldn't face anyone. Francesca came to fetch her back — it was unacceptable to leave during a meal — but Alison yelled through her locked door that she was not feeling well and the cook had gone away.

Zoey had come tapping on her door, too, twice. But Alison wasn't ready to talk. She wasn't even ready to get out of bed to unlock the door.

"I'll call you," she'd said feebly, hoping Zoey would understand.

All night she had tossed and turned, replaying the call with her dad in her head. *"We'll fight this,"* he'd said. But by now she knew better than to believe he could.

It seemed like she had barely fallen asleep when there came an insistent rapping at the bedroom door.

"Rise and shine," Louise, her grandmother's housekeeper, called. "We have packing to do."

Half asleep, Alison stumbled to the door and opened it a crack.

"Your grandmother's orders," Louise said apologetically. She held up a large suitcase. Two of her helpers held more luggage in the hall.

"Today? Now?" Alison blinked.

Louise nodded, and when she pushed the door open wider Alison did not stop her. "Mrs. Diamond said there's no time like the present, especially since you're on Thanksgiving break."

Right. She was on vacation. And her grandmother never wasted any time. Why not kick her to the curb today? She'd had almost eighteen hours to get used to the idea.

Pulling a fuzzy robe over her Juicy sweats, Alison cinched the belt tightly before walking slowly down the grand staircase to the dining room. Her grandmother did not like her to come to the table in her pajamas. But since she wasn't staying . . .

"You slept late," Tamara announced as Alison came in.

Not much to get up for, Alison thought, taking her seat. "I wasn't feeling well," she said.

A soft-boiled egg waited in a porcelain egg cup on Alison's plate. Ugh. Alison hated soft-boiled eggs. The yolks were too drippy. She took a slice of wheat toast from the platter between her and her grandmother. It was cold. But it was the only other food on the table, and since she had not touched a bite of Thanksgiving dinner, she needed something to keep her stomach from eating itself.

"I did not appreciate your behavior yesterday," Grandmother Diamond addressed Alison in the clipped tone she usually reserved for servants and animals. "I was very disappointed." As she spoke she tapped a ring around the shell of her egg with her spoon and lifted the top off.

"I'm sorry I left the table." Alison tried not to cringe as she watched her grandmother spoon up a runny bite of egg. "I wasn't well," she repeated softly. The voice in her head screamed, *Why are you doing this to me?*

"It was very rude." Tamara spooned up another slimy bite without taking her eyes off of Alison.

As rude as throwing me out of the house in front of a roomful of guests? Alison dared herself to say the words aloud but couldn't. All that came out was another apology. "I know, Grandmother. I'm sorry."

Lifting up her egg in its little cup, Alison set it next to her plate. Suddenly, as much as she was dreading going to Kelly's house, she wanted to leave the Diamond Estate. Every second she had to spend at her grandmother's was torture.

Why are you punishing me? she wanted to ask. *I did everything you asked. I chose you over my own mother!*

"Did I disappoint you during the trial, Grandmother?" Alison asked softly.

"Of course not." Tamara sprinkled coarse sea salt onto her gaping egg.

"I mean, I hope I haven't upset you in some way. . . ." Alison knew she was acting desperate now, but she couldn't leave without an answer.

Grandmother Diamond set down her spoon, creating a yellow stain on the white china. "Do you feel that I owe you something, Alison?" she asked. "It seems to me I have been very generous."

"Of course." Alison struggled to swallow the dry bite of toast in her mouth. It felt like a Brillo pad scouring the inside of her cheeks.

"Thank you, Grandmother." She gulped, letting the toast scrape down her throat. "Thank you for everything."

Chapter Thirty-seven

The drive between the Diamond Estate and the Reeves house was much too short. In no time Fernando was leaving Alison's grandmother's street with its stately mansions and pulling closer to where Kelly and her family lived. The people and the houses in the Reeves' part of town all looked the same — like fresh money. Alison wished she could instruct Fernando to take her somewhere, anywhere else.

"Here we are." Fernando pulled the car into the Reeves' wide drive. A moment later the automatic gates opened and he drove in, stopping near the front door. He looked at Alison over the seat and for a second she thought the driver was going to tell her he was sorry to see her go. "Your new home sweet home," he said instead.

"Right," Alison sighed. There was nothing sweet about it. She sat where she was, slouched in the backseat, and waited for Fernando to open the door. Usually she got her own door, but today she just didn't have the energy. Besides, she was in no hurry.

Kelly's house was big, two stories with a huge basement that they used as a giant family game room. Back when she and Kelly were friends, Alison used to dream of living there. When she and Kelly were little, they had sleepovers every weekend and begged their moms to let Alison move in so they would never have to be separated.

The memory hurt. She and Kelly had been through a lot since then, and Alison doubted they could ever find a way back to where they had been. Still, a tiny piece of her dared to wonder if living under the same roof would be a step in the right direction. If she was thinking about the past, maybe Kelly was as well. Kelly might remember how good they had been together — back when they were a team.

"Here you go." Fernando held the door open with one hand. In the other he had the largest of the suitcases Louise had packed.

"Here I go." Alison stood up and took a deep breath. "Wish me luck," she said to Fernando before ringing the doorbell.

A musical chime sounded inside. Alison stood up straighter just as Aunt Phoebe opened the door.

"Welcome!" Alison's aunt held her arms wide and Alison tolerated an awkward hug. "We are so happy to have you," Phoebe said, patting Alison's back like she was trying to make the sentiment stick. "Aren't we, Kelly?" Phoebe stepped back, motioning with one arm for Kelly to come out of the kitchen.

"Oh, yes." Kelly stepped into the entry, blocking Fernando, who was now struggling under the weight of three large cases. "We are *so* happy to have you. We're going to have such *fun*." The smile on Kelly's face was so forced and cold it gave Alison a chill. She wrapped her cashmere

Michael Kors peacoat more tightly around herself. The icy threat behind the words came through loud and clear.

"I put you in the room right next to Kelly's," Aunt Phoebe said, oblivious to the tension between the two girls. She took Alison's hand and led her toward it. "I think you'll be very comfortable there. It doesn't have its own bath, but the one down the hall is all yours. Kelly has her own, of course, so you won't have to share with anyone."

Never letting go of her hand, Aunt Phoebe dragged Alison around the familiar house like she was showing it to her for the first time. "We want you to think of this as *home*," she kept saying.

Yippee.

"I've made some cookies — oatmeal chocolate chip — your favorite," Phoebe said. "Let's go into the —"

"I think I'd like to be alone," Alison said.

"Of course, dear. Whatever you want." Phoebe smiled, but Alison could see the disappointment on her face. She followed Alison down the hall to her room and stood in the doorway, not moving. "It's just so good to have you here."

"Do you mind if I . . ." Alison grasped the door handle and inched it closer to her aunt.

"Oh! Oh, yes, sorry." Phoebe took a step backward into the hall so Alison could shut the door but still didn't leave. She just stood there smiling away.

When the door clicked shut at last Alison collapsed backward onto the queen-size bed with the delicate flowered duvet and stared up at the French blue ceiling. Aunt Phoebe had used her mother's line of decorator paint, of course, and had opted for white walls and a colored ceiling. The chaise lounge and cushion on the vanity bench matched the ceiling perfectly. Helen Rose would be proud.

Alison sighed. She was finally alone. Alone in the last place she wanted to be. *This is what I get for betraying my mother,* she thought miserably. *It's exactly what I deserve.* But she was not sure she could take it.

Sitting up, Alison looked at the bags piled around the large guest room.

Spotting her overnight case in the corner —

the only bag she had packed herself — Alison picked it up and put it on the bed. Unzipping it, she pulled out her Lulu Guinness travel roll with its black-and-white key-to-my-heart design. She opened it on the bed. She unsnapped one of the smaller pockets and pulled out the object she was looking for, a small cloisonné box, and flipped it open. Aunt Christine's Harry Winston diamond earrings sparkled up at her — the ones Alison had stolen and blamed on Kelly. Just seeing them made Alison feel a tiny bit better. If things got unbearable, she could always cash them in for her ticket out of here — two shiny escape hatches, just in case.

Chapter Thirty-eight

Kelly shut the door to her bedroom firmly but quietly. It was tempting to slam it, to jar Alison and upset her mother, but Kelly knew that was too immature, and too predictable. Better to leave Alison alone for now and let her wait, wondering when Kelly might strike. The idea of pathetic little Alison holed up in the guest room, shaking like a cornered mouse, brought warmth to Kelly's heart. She would deal with her cousin later. Right now she had someone more pressing to strike back at — Dustin.

Seething, Kelly sat down hard at her desk. She pushed a button on her black MacBook and waited for it to boot up. "Come on," she whispered impatiently. In another minute she had launched her browser and was pulling up secured account information.

She practically laughed aloud when she thought about how stupid Dustin had been to give her his account information. Then again, he had not exactly been winning any genius awards lately. Revenge would be a snap. The same numbers he'd given her to transfer funds into his account were all she needed to empty it out completely.

When her phone rang Kelly grabbed it, annoyed at the interruption. The name on the tiny screen turned her scowl into a smile. Chad.

She spun her chair away from the computer and flipped the Razr open. "Hey! I was just thinking about you," she purred into the phone.

"You were, huh? You must be psychic. Where's that money you promised me?"

What the — Kelly held the phone away from her ear and stared at it. The name on the screen was Chad's, but the voice on the other end was Dustin's. Quickly recovering from the shock, Kelly realized the timing of the call was actually perfect.

"I'm working on it right now." She turned calmly back to her computer screen, pinching the phone between her shoulder and head so her hands were free to tap the last few digits she needed into the keyboard.

"You are? That's great," Dustin burbled.

Kelly smiled to herself and pressed enter. "There, you're all taken care of," she cooed. In two seconds his account would be drained. He'd had just enough money in there to pay her back . . . with interest.

If he weren't Chad's big brother, Kelly would strike back much harder. But this revenge would teach Dustin a much needed lesson. And losing the cash would hit Dustin a lot harder than it had hit her.

"Thanks, Kelly." Dustin sounded elated. "You're the best."

"I know," Kelly answered, closing her phone with the satisfaction of knowing that this was the last time Dustin would mess with a Diamond. "And don't you forget it."

Chapter Thirty-nine

"Come in," Chad replied to the soft knock on his bedroom door. It was Saturday morning, and he was going through his stuff with a vengeance. Something amazing had happened when he woke up that morning. For the first time since the coma, he felt like himself — and knew exactly who he was.

The door opened and Tom stepped inside. "Whoa, dude," he said, glancing around Chad's room. "It looks like a tornado blew through this place."

"Tom!" Chad cried, shoving old notebooks and pictures off his lap and scrambling to his feet. "Tom, it's back! My memory is back!" He

192

threw his arms around his friend so hard he nearly knocked him over. "I can't tell you how good it feels. I'm back!"

"Hey, congratulations," Tom said. But he sounded less than psyched. Chad looked at his best friend. Tom's brow was furrowed and he stood with his hands shoved into his pockets and his shoulders hunched. He looked almost . . . nervous.

"So, uh, you remember our fight?" Tom asked quietly.

Chad shook his head. "Actually, I don't. I can't remember anything from the past few months. My doctor said I may never regain that. But everything else is back."

Chad sank onto his bed. He'd been going through stuff all morning, and it had wiped him out. "I get to go back to school on Monday."

Tom nodded. "That's great, man, really great."

"I never thought I'd be this excited about school. But I can't wait to just do something normal. Once the chemo starts . . ." He trailed off.

Tom shifted uncomfortably.

"Hey, Tom?" Chad blurted. "There are a couple of things I need to ask you . . . about Kelly . . . and Alison." Tom finally met his eyes, then pulled out Chad's desk chair and sat down.

Chad scooted back so he was sitting against the pillows on his bed. This was the one thing that had been bothering him: Alison and Kelly. Maybe Tom could help him figure it out. "I remember Alison now," Chad said. "I remember how it was when we were together. How amazing she was. I don't remember our breakup, but . . . the thing is, I just can't see her doing all those things that Kelly says she did." Chad sat up, leaning toward Tom. "Kelly told me she broke up with me when she found out about Will, then tried to get me back later by ruining Kelly's rep. But it just . . . I mean, did she really? Tom, I need the truth."

Chapter Forty

Tom stared down at the old yearbooks and trophies and photos scattered across Chad's floor. Right next to his feet there was a photo strip of Chad and Alison, their faces stuck together and their smiles bright. A gold-framed photo of Chad and Kelly at the fall formal lay next to it.

Tom swallowed hard and looked up. Chad's eyes were the clearest he had seen them since he'd come out of his coma, and they were searching Tom's face, waiting for an answer.

Problem was, the answer would send Chad right back into Alison's arms. And with Alison was exactly where Tom wanted to be. More than anything. Part of Tom wanted to tell Chad that Alison had done those things, just so he could have a chance to have her for himself. But that wasn't fair to Alison, or to Chad. And he'd already decided he would be a true friend to Chad from now on.

"No," Tom said, shaking his head, "she didn't. You dumped Alison. You dumped her for Kelly. Alison never tried to get you back. And she never met Will — she didn't even know you had a little brother until Kelly told her. By then you were already in the coma." Tom gulped, thinking about everything Alison had been through. He remembered how sad and confused she'd seemed after Kelly had told her about Will. She couldn't understand why her boyfriend had kept such an important secret from her. She had looked so sad.

Because she really cares about Chad, Tom realized. *Because she's still in love with him.* He wanted to kick himself. *No wonder she ran away from me at Thanksgiving. I was such an idiot.*

"Alison isn't like that," Tom said, feeling a hollow ache in his chest. "She's just as sweet as she seems. She's . . . amazing."

Chad stared at Tom as the information slowly sank in. "But Kelly —"

"Kelly played us," Tom finally said. There was no other way to explain it. "She played us both, and I'm just sorry I let her come between us."

Chad blinked and sat back, silent. Then, after a minute, he sat up again. "But we're really together — me and Kelly? I mean, am I really into her?"

Tom almost laughed aloud.

"Definitely. You can't believe your luck. But," he added, knowing he had to be completely honest, "it isn't like what I — I mean, what *you* had with Alison."

"That's what I thought," Chad murmured, flopping back onto the pillows and sending a flock of photos fluttering to the carpet. He looked wiped out, but he also looked happy. And there was a new look about him that Tom hadn't seen since he'd woken up from his coma — relief. "Alison is what's been coming back the strongest — how awesome she is. How great we were together." He turned to Tom, his eyes sparkling. "I can't wait to tell her. I have to make things right."

Chad swung his feet over the edge of the bed. "Don't look so down," he said, punching Tom on the shoulder. "I forgive you, man. I completely forgive you. So let's make a pact," Chad said earnestly. "Let's promise to never let a girl come between us again."

Tom broke eye contact and stared at the floor, where his heart was lying among the memorabilia. Chad was really back, and all was forgiven. But now that all was well? All was terrible. The one person he longed to be with was, once again, his best friend's girl. He had to tell him.

"What is it?" Chad asked, searching his face.

Tom looked up at his friend and forced a smile. "Nothing," he lied. "Nothing at all."

Chapter Forty-one

"That was fast," Zoey murmured to herself. She closed the journal she had been writing in and got up to open the door. Alison had called less than fifteen minutes earlier to ask if she could come over — and had obviously gotten across town in record time.

"How bad is it?" Zoey asked as she opened the heavy wooden door. One look at her best friend and she knew the answer. It was beyond bad. "Oh, Al." Zoey grabbed Alison by the arm and led her up to her room.

When the door was shut behind them Alison flopped down on the bed with a groan. "I'm suf-focating. Aunt Phoebe is acting like I'm her own

199

personal teddy bear or something," Alison griped. "She's constantly hugging me and telling me how happy they are to have me with them. As if," she added, rolling her eyes. "Kelly is ignoring me completely, which is actually worse than her trademark nastiness. It makes me feel . . ." She looked up at Zoey, her eyes glistening. "Invisible."

Zoey sat down on the bed and slung an arm around her friend. "Oh, Alison, I'm so sorry," she said. She knew that Helen Rose's personal form of parental torture had been making Alison feel as though she didn't exist. And it had left a big open wound.

Wiping her cheek, Alison smiled through her tears. "Thanks," she said. "I don't know what I'd do without you — and your safe house."

Zoey grinned. "You can hang out as long as you want," she said, getting to her feet. "Dad and Deirdre are out until tonight, and Tom is with Chad. I'd stay with you, but I promised the Wilsons I'd help them finish Audra's room. And the sooner I'm done with that little job, the better," she added with a sigh. She couldn't wait to be released of her Audra duties. She had promised herself that this was the last time she'd visit.

Quickly Zoey shoved a few things into her messenger bag, keeping an eye on Alison. Her friend was biting her lip, and her eyes were seriously welling with tears. "I can be late, though," she added, sitting back down. "C'mon, spill it."

Alison wiped her face on her sleeve and sighed. "Ugh. I hate this," she murmured. She was quiet for a moment, thinking. Then she looked up at Zoey and started to explain. "I can live with Kelly — she's probably no worse than what I deserve. The thing I can't live with is . . . what I did. To my mom. I sold her out, Zoey. I'm no better than my grandmother — or Kelly or my aunt Christine." Alison's shoulders shook with the sobs she was fighting to keep in. "And I can't be like them," she whispered. "I just can't."

Zoey gave Alison's hand a squeeze, then got to her feet and walked around to the side of her bed. She reached between the mattress and the box spring and pulled out a plain manila envelope — the same envelope Alison had given Zoey right after she'd stolen it from her grandmother's vault.

"So I guess you'll be needing this," she said, tossing the evidence onto her duvet.

Alison picked up the envelope, her hand shaking slightly. The tears disappeared and she straightened her shoulders. "I guess I will," she agreed.

Chapter Forty-two

"You can tell us what happened that afternoon whenever you're ready," Beverly Wilson said in a soft, low voice. "We promise not to push. Whenever you're ready . . ."

She'd make a great hypnotist, Zoey thought. She could not count how many times Beverly had asked her to talk about Audra's death, or how many times she had avoided replaying that horrible sequence of events. She wished the Wilsons would let it go. But she understood why they couldn't, too. She knew what it was like. How losing someone so abruptly was like having your heart cut out. How desperate you were for answers.

She'd come here to say good-bye, to tell them she couldn't keep coming. Except, she hadn't managed to tell them yet. . . .

"I'm just going to take these downstairs." Zoey stood up from the floor and picked up two of the handled bags filled with Audra's stuff and marked for donation. She needed a second to breathe.

Downstairs by the front door, Zoey dropped the bags next to some others that were waiting for pickup. She inhaled slowly, preparing to go back up and finish what she had begun with the Wilsons. But as she turned around she noticed an open door just off the front entry — Douglas Wilson's office.

Zoey tiptoed into the darkened room. The blinds were closed, so only two slits of light came in from outside. When her eyes adjusted, Zoey saw pretty much what she expected from a shrink's office. An Eames chair. A red upholstered modern couch. A Scandinavian-looking table. Some weird art pieces that probably worked like Rorschach ink blots to stimulate conversation. And just to the left of the door she saw several filing cabinets.

Dr. Wilson had been her mom's psychiatrist. Which meant he had records . . .

Listening for footsteps on the stairs, Zoey pulled out the drawer with the label R-S-T. There, right in front, was exactly what she was looking for — a folder marked *S. Ramirez*.

I can't believe I'm doing this. Holding her breath, Zoey slipped the file out of the drawer and stepped back into the hall. Quickly she stashed it in one of the donation bags before hurrying back up the stairs. She had to get back before Beverly and Douglas missed her.

"I can take the donation stuff and drop it off," Zoey offered, hoping she sounded more innocent than she felt.

"That's so nice," Beverly answered. When her eyes met Zoey's, Zoey did not feel nice. She felt lousy. *Just tell them*, Zoey suddenly thought. *Tell them what really happened so they can move on, and you can be done with it. Tell them, and then leave.* It was the least she could do, really.

"Beverly" — Zoey took a deep breath — "I think I'm ready to tell you now." She sank down to her knees so she was sitting near Audra's mom on the floor, in Audra's room, and began to talk.

Chapter Forty-three

Alison sat alone in Zoey's room, flipping through her grandmother's documents.

Just having the evidence on the floor in front of her made Alison's heart pound, but she also felt relieved. After months of indecision, and even now when it seemed too late, she'd made up her mind. She had decided to help her mother and knew for sure that it was the right thing to do. *Monday morning,* she told herself. *On Monday I'll take this to Mother's lawyers.*

Slipping the papers back into the envelope and sealing the clasp, Alison got to her feet. She should probably get going, but there was another reason she had wanted to come over to Zoey's. . . .

Alison walked down the hall, stopping outside the door to Tom's room. It wasn't latched. Pushing it open, she quickly stepped inside and closed it behind her. The room smelled familiar — clean and soapy, like Tom. Alison took a deep breath and sat down on the bed. There was so much of Tom to look at in here, and being surrounded by his stuff was comforting, almost like being back in her old room with all of her old stuff — only way less girly. His collection of lacrosse and swimming trophies lined the shelf in his closet, a humble display that could easily be hidden from view. Next to his bed was a giant pile of graphic novels — a testament to his lighter side — a side Alison hadn't seen much of lately and wanted to see again.

Everything just kept changing. Things had been so good when she and Chad were together. They had been happy, really happy. But Chad didn't need her now. And he didn't want her, not even as he prepared for a tough battle with cancer. That relationship was gone, and there was no going back. There was only forward.

Alison flopped back on the bed, overwhelmed. Her head landed next to a cast-off sweatshirt. Tom's sweatshirt. Sitting back up, Alison grabbed it and pulled it on over her head. She breathed it in, inhaling the wonderful clean smell that was Tom.

What am I doing? She half wondered if she was becoming a crazy stalker like Audra. *No. I'm doing what I should have done a long time ago — I'm taking care of myself.* Hugging the manila envelope to her chest and keeping the sweatshirt on, Alison stood up and tiptoed out of Tom's room.

Her mind was doubly made up now. Alison felt stronger than she had in a long time. She was done being a doormat. It was time to go after something for herself . . . and get it.

And what Alison wanted was Tom.

Chapter Forty-four

Numbers swam in front of Chad's eyes. After the euphoria of his returned memory came the harsh reality of catching up on everything he had missed — namely, his schoolwork. Tom had dropped off all the make-up material plus the homework they had been assigned for the break. *I'm never going to get through all of this!* Chad thought. How could he? He didn't remember anything he'd learned all year! Then an even scarier thought crossed his mind. *I'm going to lose my scholarship.* He had been struggling to keep up for a long time, and after all he had been through, he was determined not to start cheating again. *It isn't worth it,* he told himself. Tom said that Stafford was going to cut Chad some slack, maybe even assign him a tutor. But with all the catching up he had to do, plus chemo on the side . . . keeping up seemed impossible.

What I need is a relationship *tutor.*

Monday was not going to be easy, and not just because of the schoolwork. Chad had decided he had to talk to Kelly before then, and in person. What he had to say was too important not to say it face to face.

"Hey." Chad's door opened and Dustin stepped into the mess, knocking on the dresser top only after he was inside.

"Come in," Chad joked.

"I, uh, just wanted to say good-bye," Dustin said.

"You just got here." Chad was confused. Thanksgiving dinner had gone amazingly well — there was no yelling at all. And Dustin had even come over for leftovers the next day without incident. After two good days in a row Chad had been half expecting him to say he was moving back in. "Where are you going? I'm starting chemo next week. Aren't you going to stick around for that?"

"Things have changed. I need to take off." Dustin shuffled the mess on the floor around with his feet. He didn't look Chad in the eye.

"All right, *bro*," Chad mocked him. "Thanks for being here."

"Don't be like that," Dustin said quietly. "It's bad timing is all. My investment deal fell through and some people are looking for me. I need to lay low and earn a little money somewhere else."

Neither brother spoke for what felt like a long time. Chad was seething. Along with the rest of his memory had come the memories of Dustin's stupid schemes. He had gotten himself in so deep he had to bail out.

"You're gonna be okay." Dustin sat down on the corner of Chad's bed. "But seriously, there is something I need to warn you about."

Great, more brotherly advice, Chad thought. If Dustin really cared, he would stick around to help and not just run from his own problems.

"Your girlfriend . . . Kelly —"

Chad interrupted the second he saw where Dustin was going. "Don't bother. I don't need your advice." Chad turned away. "Kelly isn't the girl for me."

Dustin looked up, suddenly curious. "No? And who is?" he asked.

"Alison," Chad said confidently.

Dustin laughed a short barking laugh, then got up to go. "You're gonna be all right, little bro," he said with a smirk. "Just fine, in fact." He laughed again, then disappeared out the door.

Chapter Forty-five

Kelly was sleeping deeply when her phone rang. She fumbled for it on the bedside table, felt it, and answered without even opening her eyes. "What?" she demanded groggily.

"I'm leaving town, Reeves."

Kelly's eyes popped open and her breath caught in her throat. The deep voice was unmistakable. She looked at the glowing numbers on her clock. It was after midnight.

"But don't think you've heard the last of me," Dustin snarled. "Not by a long shot."

"Don't threaten me," Kelly said, propping herself up on one elbow and trying to keep her voice cool. "And don't call me again. Ever," she said, waking up enough to feel furious.

"You're just lucky Chad cares about you," she hissed into the phone. "Or I wouldn't stop at just evening the score."

There was a long throaty laugh on the other end of the line. "So I guess you haven't heard the good news." Dustin's tone was mocking.

Kelly bit. "What news?"

"Chad got his memory back," Dustin replied cheerily. "He remembers everything, including the girl he really loves."

Barely breathing, Kelly waited to see if Dustin would say more.

He did. "Alison."

There was a click and the line went dead. Kelly felt frozen, unsure what to believe. Dustin was a liar. But he sounded so happy, he could just be telling the truth. And if he was . . . the love of her boyfriend's life was sleeping in the room next door.

Chapter Forty-six

Rolling over in his dark bedroom, Tom pulled his pillow over his head and yelled into the mattress in frustration. *What is wrong with me?* he wondered. *Why is my timing so bad?*

Tom knew he should be glad that Chad's life was falling back into place. It was great for his best friend. It was great for Alison. And Tom wanted the world for her. For them. But it hurt. The knowledge that he couldn't have Alison for himself made his whole body feel heavy. He wished he could just sink into his mattress, never to emerge.

He tried to block out everything — the sound

of the wind outside, the ticking of the clock on his nightstand, his ringing phone . . .

What? Tom pushed his pillow aside and picked up his phone. He had forgotten to turn it off. It was probably a wrong number.

The number was blocked. "Hello?"

"Hello, Thomas, did I wake you?"

"Um. No." Tom rubbed his eyes with his free hand. "Who is this?" The voice was a girl's, and she sounded familiar. But it wasn't Alison. Or Kelly.

"It's me. X." She laughed.

Tom found himself smiling. X had an excellent laugh, light and infectious. It made Tom feel like he was in on a really good joke. But where did she get his number? And why was she calling in the middle of the night? "Hey, what's going on?" Tom asked, sitting up.

"We are," X replied. "When are you going to take me out?"

Chapter Forty-seven

"*What?*" Alison shouted, knowing it was useless. Her dad was sitting behind the thick prison glass in the visiting area. She could see his mouth moving but couldn't hear his words. And he could not hear hers, either. She pressed up against the glass and watched his lips closely. If she could just read them . . .

"*Unlock it,*" he mouthed. He held his fingers together and turned them, like he was turning a small key. The key!

Alison's hands flew to her throat. She sat bolt upright and woke up. She was in bed at Kelly's house, in what she thought of as the "unwanted guest" room. And she had been dreaming.

It was a dream, she told herself. Still, Alison's heart hammered. It had seemed so real. Her dad. The prison. The key. They did not go together, but in her dream they'd made perfect sense. If only he'd been able to tell her what the key unlocked.

Unclasping the chain that held the tiny key, Alison dangled it in front of her own eyes. It was barely visible in the dark room. She dropped the key and chain into her opposite palm and closed her fist around them. Then she flipped on the light beside her bed and checked the time. 2:15. She was wide awake and it wouldn't be morning for hours. Pulling her knees to her chest, she wrapped her arms around them. She had plenty of time to think about the key now.

For a minute Alison just sat. She propped her chin on her knees and shivered, happy to be wrapped in Tom's big fleecy shirt. She hadn't really meant to steal it. She just wanted a little bit of Tom to take with her — a little piece of the feeling she used to get when they sat together and talked. But now that she had it, she was not sure how to explain it. "Hi, I'm Alison, I'll be your new stalker. . . ."

Groaning silently, Alison got out of bed. There was nothing she could do about that now. She couldn't exactly call Tom at 2 A.M. and apologize for pilfering his shirt. But she could write her dad another letter and try to get to the bottom of the key mystery.

Alison flipped on the desk light and pulled opened the top drawer. It was stocked, of course, with stationery, nice pens, and even stamps. *Welcome to Phoebe Reeves's B&B.* Alison sat down and was about to begin writing when she noticed an antique-looking box on the desk she had overlooked before. It was pretty, hand-painted with a Japanese motif. The edges were silver, but what caught Alison's eye was the tiny lock. It looked like the right size. . . .

No way.

With trembling hands, Alison tried the key. It slipped into the lock easily and when she turned it she heard a soft click. The top opened! Alison peered inside and slowly removed the contents — a single folded piece of paper. Opening it, she began to read:

Certificate of Live Birth.

Child: Jeremy Diamond Jones.

Alison gasped. *Diamond? Jeremy?* She skipped several lines and kept reading.

Mother: Honey Helen Diamond.

Father: Harris Tate Jones.

It couldn't be! But here in her hands was the proof.

"Up late, Alison?"

Alison pressed the paper to her chest as she whirled around to see Kelly standing behind her. She had been so engrossed in what she was reading that she hadn't even heard her cousin come in.

"Doing a little late-night reading?" Kelly purred. And before Alison could stop her, she reached out and snatched the birth certificate from her hands.

Take a peek at the final book
in the Little Secrets series,
Lock and Key!

It all comes down to this...

The drama continues in
book six, *Lock and Key*.
Here's a sneak peek.

When the large entrance to the café opened
again, Chad blew in with a gust of chilly air. Kelly's
pulse quickened. Though he'd lost quite a bit of
weight in the hospital, the color was back in his
cheeks. His curls had been tousled by the wind,
his brown eyes were shining, and he looked better than he had in a long time. Maybe even
better than chocolate.

"Hey," Chad greeted as he loped to the table
where Kelly was waiting. He bent over and kissed
her cheek before moving her parka and sitting
down across from her. "Hope you weren't waiting long. My mom didn't think I should go out in
the cold." He sounded a little winded.

"Not too long." Kelly smiled, trying to catch Chad's eye. He hadn't looked her in the face since he walked in. And now, unwinding his knit scarf from around his neck, he was looking at the floor. Something *was* up. As the waiter approached the table, Kelly decided to chalk Chad's behavior up to nerves. After all, he was starting his chemotherapy this week, and it sounded pretty nasty.

"What can I get you two?" the young waiter asked. He said "two," but his eyes were resting solely on Kelly. He didn't even take his gaze off her face to write things down. *This is more like it,* Kelly thought. She was used to this kind of attention. So why wasn't she getting it from her boyfriend?

When their order was in, Kelly leaned across the small round table and grabbed Chad's hand. "Now tell me what I can get for *you*." She looked intently into Chad's face. He couldn't avoid her gaze now, and she felt him studying her green eyes before he turned away.

"This is really hard to say." Chad gazed down at his hands and shook his head. When he looked back up he said, a little too loudly, "Kelly, I think you're a really great girl."

Kelly dropped Chad's hand and sat back in her chair. Dustin was right after all . . . he was breaking up with her! *Chad* was breaking up with *her*! "Who is it?" Kelly demanded, trying to keep the anger out of her voice. Deep inside she was praying that Dustin had not been right about *everything*.

Chad sighed. "Nobody. I mean, I do have feelings for someone else, but she doesn't know it." Chad started to trail off before finding his voice again. "Kel, I want you to know I am really grateful to you for standing by me during the coma and all . . . I just, I don't think we should be together."

At that moment, the waiter came back. He placed a nonfat, double mocha (no whip) in front of Kelly, and a gourmet chocolate chip cookie and a shot of cold frothy milk in front of Chad. Kelly swirled the mocha with a wooden stick and pursed her lips. She wasn't sure what she was more upset about, Chad dumping her or Dustin telling the truth — and knowing before she did.

"So, you're breaking up with me?" she asked. The cute waiter who had been staring before looked back at Kelly and winked. In an instant, Kelly remembered who she was and how much she could have — without anyone's help.

Chad was not just breaking up with her, he was doing her a huge favor. Once again, the world was wide open. The possibilities were endless.

Confidence intact, she grabbed the wheel and began steering the wayward conversation in a new direction. There was still one thing she had to know.

"Is it Alison?" Kelly asked. Chad went white. It was all the answer she needed.

Kelly pondered this information for half a second. Alison would probably think she had won this round and the guy they had been playing tug-of-war with. But what exactly was Alison winning? Her sickly leftovers? The thought made Kelly bite her lip to hide a smile. Alison could have them.

"I'm really sorry, Kelly. I wanted to tell you in person," Chad was starting to babble awkwardly.

Was he actually afraid Kelly was going to start crying?

Kelly leaned in close and put her finger over Chad's lips to shush him. Locking Chad in her green-eyed gaze, she smiled her brilliant, bitter-sweet, Kelly smile — the one that started at one corner of her mouth and slowly worked its way to the other side while her eyes remained full of concern. "Oh, Chad," she said. "I'm so relieved. I was hoping you'd be the first one to say it . . ."

To Do List: Read all the Point books!

By Aimee Friedman

- ☐ South Beach
- ☐ French Kiss
- ☐ Hollywood Hills
- ☐ The Year My Sister Got Lucky

- ☐ Oh Baby!
  By Randi Reisfeld and H.B. Gilmour

. . . .

- ☐ Hotlanta
  By Denene Millner and Mitzi Miller

By Hailey Abbott

- ☐ Summer Boys
- ☐ Next Summer: A Summer Boys Novel
- ☐ After Summer: A Summer Boys Novel
- ☐ Last Summer: A Summer Boys Novel

By Claudia Gabel

- ☐ In or Out
- ☐ Loves Me, Loves Me Not: An In or Out Novel
- ☐ Sweet and Vicious: An In or Out Novel

By Nina Malkin

- ☐ 6X: The Uncensored Confessions
- ☐ 6X: Loud, Fast, & Out of Control
- ☐ Orange Is the New Pink

By Jeanine Le Ny

- ☐ Once Upon a Prom: Date
- ☐ Once Upon a Prom: Dress
- ☐ Once Upon a Prom: Dream

SCHOLASTIC and associated logos are trademarks and/or registered trademarks of Scholastic Inc.

I ♥ Bikinis series

❏ I ♥ Bikinis:
He's with Me
By Tamara Summers

❏ I ♥ Bikinis:
Island Summer
By Jeanine Le Ny

❏ I ♥ Bikinis:
What's Hot
By Caitlyn Davis

❏ Pool Boys
By Erin Haft

❏ Rewind
By Laura Dower

❏ To Catch a Pirate
By Jade Parker

❏ Kissing Snowflakes
By Abby Sher

❏ The Heartbreakers
By Pamela Wells

❏ Secret Santa
By Sabrina James

By Emily Blake

❏ Little Secrets 1: Playing
with Fire

❏ Little Secrets 2: No
Accident

❏ Little Secrets 3: Over
the Edge

Story Collections

❏ Fireworks: Four
Summer Stories
By Niki Burnham, Erin
Haft, Sarah Mlynowski,
and Lauren Myracle

❏ 21 Proms
Edited by Daniel Ehrenhaft
and David Levithan

❏ Mistletoe: Four
Holiday Stories
By Hailey Abbott,
Melissa de la Cruz, Aimee
Friedman, and Nina Malkin

Point

www.thisispoint.com